'Why did you come here this evening, really?'

Charlotte swallowed. Her skin felt tight and hot and her mouth was dry. Her heart was beating like a trapped bird against her chest. 'Just as I told you… I wanted to make sure you knew that I don't…don't have romantic notions.'

The wind screeched outside. Salim's eyes were like two blue flames. 'Believe me, the last thing you inspire is feelings of romance. You inspire much earthier things. Dark and decadent things.'

There was still a couple of feet between them but Charlotte felt as if Salim was touching her. The push and pull inside her was torture. For a second she almost took a step towards him, giving in to the inexorable pull.

Before she could lose her mind completely, she blurted out, 'I'm going back to my tent.'

She turned abruptly and blindly felt for the opening of the tent. Panic mounted, and then she heard Salim's voice.

'We're in the middle of a storm. The tent has been secured for our safety.'

Charlotte almost couldn't articulate the words, but she forced them out. 'So, what does that mean..?'

An unmistakable glint of something wicked in Salim's eyes replaced any hint of innocence on his har... have to s...

A CHRISTMAS BRIDE FOR THE KING

BY

ABBY GREEN

MILLS & BOON

All rights reserved including the right of reproduction in whole and or in part in any form. This edition is published by arrangement with Harle...

This is a work of fiction. Names, characters, places, locations and incidents are purely fictional and bear no relationship to any real life individuals, living or dead, or to any actual places, business establishments, locations, events or incidents. Any resemblance is entirely coincidental.

This book is sold subject to the condition that it shall not, by way of trade or otherwise, be lent, resold, hired out or otherwise circulated without the prior consent of the publisher in any form of binding or cover other than that in which it is published and without a similar condition including this condition being imposed on the subsequent purchaser.

® and TM are trademarks owned and used by the trademark owner and/or its licensee. Trademarks marked with ® are registered with the United Kingdom Patent Office and/or the Office for Harmonisation in the Internal Market and in other countries.

First Published in Great Britain 2017
By Mills & Boon, an imprint of HarperCollins*Publishers*
1 London Bridge Street, London, SE1 9GF

© 2017 Abby Green

ISBN: 978-0-263-92494-7

Our policy is to use papers that are natural, renewable and recyclable products and made from wood grown in sustainable forests. The logging and manufacturing processes conform to the legal environmental regulations of the country of origin.

Printed and bound in Spain
by CPI, Barcelona

Irish author **Abby Green** threw in a very glamorous career in film and TV—which really consisted of a lot of standing in the rain outside actors' trailers—to pursue her love of romance. After she'd bombarded Mills & Boon with manuscripts they kindly accepted one, and an author was born. She lives in Dublin, Ireland, and loves any excuse for distraction. Visit abby-green.com or email abbygreenauthor@gmail.com.

Books by Abby Green

Mills & Boon Modern Romance

Awakened by Her Desert Captor

Rulers of the Desert

A Diamond for the Sheikh's Mistress

Wedlocked!

Claimed for the De Carrillo Twins

Brides for Billionaires

Married for the Tycoon's Empire

One Night With Consequences

An Heir to Make a Marriage
An Heir Fit for a King

Billionaire Brothers

Fonseca's Fury
The Bride Fonseca Needs

Blood Brothers

When Falcone's World Stops Turning
When Christakos Meets His Match
When Da Silva Breaks the Rules

Visit the Author Profile page
at millsandboon.co.uk for more titles.

This is for my Charlotte,
whose friendship has made my life
immeasurably richer in so many ways.
Thelma & Louise 4 Ever. xx

PROLOGUE

THE PUNISHINGLY HOT shower Sheikh Salim Ibn Hafiz Al-Noury had just subjected himself to had done little to dispel the hollow feeling that lingered after his less than sensually satisfying encounter with a convenient lover. It wasn't her fault. She was stunning. And, what was more important, she accepted his strict no-strings rules.

He never engaged with women who didn't, because he'd built his life around an independence he'd cultivated as far back as he could remember. Distancing himself from his own family and the heavy legacy of his birth. Distancing himself from painful memories. Distancing himself from emotional entanglements or investment, which could only lead to unbearable heartbreak.

Salim and his brother, Zafir, had been bred as coldly and calculatedly as animals bred for their coats or meat. They'd been bred to inherit neighbouring kingdoms—Jandor, the home of their father, where they'd been born and brought up along with Salim's twin sister, Sara, and Tabat, their mother's ancestral home.

The two countries had been at war for hundreds of years, but a peace agreement had been brokered when their mother, the Crown Princess of Tabat, had married the new King of Jandor and they'd pledged to have their sons eventually ruling both countries in a bid to secure peace in the region.

On the death of their father over a year ago Zafir, as the eldest, had assumed his role as King of Jandor—which had always been more of a home to him than to Salim.

But Salim had yet to assume *his* role, as King of Tabat, and the pressure to do so was mounting on all sides.

He hitched a towel around his waist, irritated that his thoughts were straying in this direction. He ignored the sting of his conscience that told him it was a situation he had to deal with.

He'd managed to avoid dealing with it for this long because he'd built up a vast empire of business concerns, ranging from real estate to media and tech industries, none of which he could easily walk away from. None of which he wanted to walk away from. And yet, if he was honest with himself, he knew he'd finally achieved a level of success and security that *could* enable him to step back—if he had to.

The steam of the shower cleared and Salim caught his reflection in the mirror. He was momentarily taken off guard by the cynical weariness etched into his face. Blue eyes stood out starkly against the darkness of his skin. Stubble lined a hard jaw. Too hard.

With no sense of satisfaction he took in the aesthetically pleasing symmetry of his features, which called to mind another set of features—the feminine version of this face. Except that face was frozen in time, at eleven years old when his twin sister had died.

A part of Salim had broken irreparably that day: his heart. And with it any illusion of invincibility or a belief that the world was a benign place. He'd lost his soul-mate when Sara had died, and he never wanted to experience that kind of excoriating pain again.

For a moment the memory of his sister's lifeless form and pale face was sharp enough to make him draw a breath. Even after all this time. Nineteen years. He had avenged her death, but instead of bringing him peace it had compounded the emptiness inside him.

Salim's hands curled around the sink so tightly that his knuckles shone white through the skin. It was only a persistent ringing noise that broke him out of the moment.

He went into the bedroom of his New York penthouse apartment and saw his phone flashing on the nightstand. As he picked it up he registered who it was and immediately felt a tightening sensation in his chest, along with a familiar mix of turbulent emotions, the strongest of which was guilt. He was tempted to let the call go to voicemail, but he knew it would only be delaying the inevitable.

He answered with a curtness arising out of that mix of emotions and memories. 'Brother. How nice to hear from you.'

Zafir made a rude sound at this less than effusive greeting. 'I've been trying to contact you for weeks. *Hell*, Salim, why are you doing this? You're making it harder for everyone—including yourself.'

Salim ignored what Zafir had said and replied, 'I believe congratulations are in order. I'm sorry I didn't make the wedding.'

Zafir sighed. 'It's not as if I really expected you to come, Salim, but it would have been nice for you to meet Kat. She wants to meet you.'

His tone made the tightness in Salim's chest intensify. He'd done such a good job of pushing Zafir away for as long as he could remember that it seemed impossible to bridge the chasm now. And why did he suddenly feel the need to?

He shut down that rogue impulse and assured himself that he owed Zafir nothing—nor his new sister-in-law, who was now Queen of Jandor.

'I don't really have time to chat, Zafir. Why did you call?'

His brother's voice hardened. 'You know exactly why I'm calling. You've shirked your duties for long enough. Officials in Tabat have been waiting for over a year for you to assume your role as king—as per the terms of our father's will.'

Before Salim could react to that succinct summary of his situation, Zafir was continuing.

'Tabat is close to descending into chaos. This isn't just about you, Salim. People will get hurt if stability isn't restored. It's time for you to take responsibility. You are king, whether you like it or not.'

Salim wanted to snarl down the phone that he was the furthest thing from a king that a man could be. He'd pursued a life far from royal politics and that closed, rarefied world. He'd never asked for this role—it had been thrust upon him before he'd even been born. His brother's acceptance of the status quo was in direct contrast to Salim's rejection of it.

Before he could say anything, Zafir went on. 'You can't avoid this, Salim. It's your destiny, and if you don't face up to that destiny you'll have blood on your hands.'

Destiny. Salim's anger dissipated as he thought bleakly of their sister's destiny. Had it been her destiny to suffer unspeakable trauma and die so young?

After what had happened to his sister Salim didn't believe in destiny. He believed you made your own destiny. And that was what he had done for his whole life—as much for himself as to honour the life his sister had lost.

He looked out over the skyline of Manhattan, where the late autumn dawn was slowly breaking, bathing everything in a soft pink glow. It was beautiful, but it left him untouched.

At that moment a falcon glided on the air outside his window, majestic and deadly, its head swivelling back and forth, looking for prey. It was a long way from its natural habitat, and yet this bird of prey had adapted to city life as well as humans had.

A memory floated back, of him and Sara in the desert with their pet falcons. Sara had lifted her hand to encourage hers to fly high, teasing Salim that his was too lazy to budge itself… She'd been so carefree, innocent…

'Salim?'

His brother's voice broke the silence and a heavy weight settled in Salim's gut. Destiny or not, he knew he couldn't keep avoiding this inheritance he'd never asked for. It had to be dealt with.

'Fine,' he said grimly. 'I will give them their coronation. Let them know that I'm coming.'

And in doing so, he assured himself silently, he would sever his ties with his so-called destiny and the past for good.

CHAPTER ONE

CHARLOTTE MCQUILLAN PACED back and forth in the empty office and looked at her watch for the umpteenth time. The king, Salim Ibn Hafiz Al-Noury—or technically the king when he was crowned in three weeks—had kept her waiting for an hour now.

It was no secret that he was probably the most reluctant king in the world, having deferred his coronation for well over a year. Long after his older brother had been crowned king of neighbouring Jandor.

She might have expected as much from the *enfant terrible* of the international billionaire playboy scene.

Charlotte knew of Sheikh Salim Ibn Hafiz Al-Noury's reputation, but only in a peripheral sense. Salacious celebrity gossip magazines were anathema to her, because she'd been the focal point of a celebrity scandal at a very young age, but even she was aware of the sheikh with the outrageous good looks, near mythical virility and his ability to turn anything he touched to gold.

His playboy exploits were matched only by his ruthless reputation and his ability to amass huge wealth and success in the many business spheres he turned his attention to.

Charlotte walked over to a nearby window that looked out over a seemingly unending sea of sand under a painfully blue sky. The sun was a blazing orb and she shivered lightly in the air-conditioning, imagining how merciless that heat must be with no shade. The little taste of it she'd had walking from the plane to the sheikh's chauffeur-driven car and then into the palace had almost felled her.

With her fair, strawberry-blonde colouring, Charlotte had never been a sun-worshipper. And yet here she was. Because when the opportunity had come up to escape London in the full throes of Christmas countdown she'd jumped at it.

To say it wasn't her favourite time of the year was an understatement. She loathed Christmas, with all its glittery twinkling lights and forced festive joviality, because this was the time of year when her world had fallen apart and she'd realised that happiness and security were just an illusion that could be ripped away at any moment.

Like the Wizard of Oz, who had appeared from behind his carefully constructed façade to reveal he wasn't a wizard at all. Far from it.

And yet as she looked out over this alien view that couldn't be more removed from that London scene, she didn't feel relieved. She felt a pang. *Worse*. A yearning.

Because in spite of everything a tiny, traitorous part of her secretly ached for the kind of Christmas celebrated in cheesy movies and on cards depicting happy families and togetherness. The fact that she usually spent her Christmas Day alone, with tears coursing down her face as she watched *Miracle On 34th Street* or *It's a Wonderful Life* for the hundredth time was a shameful secret she would take to her grave.

She made a disgusted sound at herself and turned her back on the view, firmly shoving any such rogue yearnings down deep where they belonged. She distracted herself by taking in the vast expanse of the King's Royal Office—which, if the correct protocol was being observed, she should never have been allowed into without his presence. She sighed.

She could see that at one time it had been impressive, with its huge floor-to-ceiling murals depicting scenes that looked as if they'd been plucked from a book of Arabian mythology. But now they were badly faded.

Everything Charlotte had seen so far of Tabat and its eponymous capital city had an air of faded glory and neglect. But it had charmed her with its ancient winding streets, clusters of stone buildings and the river that ran all the way from the Tabat Mountains to the sea on the coast of neighbouring Jandor.

The country was rich in natural resources—oil being the most important and lucrative. But its infrastructure was in serious need of modernisation, along with myriad other aspects of the country—education, government, economy... It badly needed a leader prepared to take on the mammoth task of hauling it into the twenty-first century. Its potential was abundant and just waiting to be tapped into.

But, from the little she knew of Sheikh Al-Noury and his reputation, she didn't hold out much hope for that happening any time soon. He'd made no secret of the fact that his priorities lay with his myriad business empires in the West.

She'd been hired by his brother, King Zafir of Jandor, to advise Salim Al-Noury on international diplomacy and relations in the run-up to his coronation, but in the two weeks since she'd accepted the assignment neither the sheikh nor his people had made any effort to return Charlotte's calls or provide her with any information.

Charlotte checked her watch again. He was now well over an hour late. Feeling frustrated, and not a little irritated and tired after her journey, she walked over to where she'd put down her document case, prepared to leave and find someone who could direct her to her room. But just as she drew near to the huge doors they swung open abruptly in her face and a man walked in.

One thing was immediately and glaringly apparent. In spite of seeing his picture online, Charlotte was not remotely prepared for Sheikh Salim Ibn Hafiz Al-Noury in the flesh. For the first time in her life she was rendered speechless.

For a start he was taller than she'd expected. Much taller. Well over six feet. And his body matched that height with broad shoulders and a wide chest narrowing down to lean hips and long legs. He was a big man, and she hadn't expected him to be so physically formidable. The impression was one of sheer force and power.

Messily tousled over-long dark hair framed his exquisitely handsome face, which was liberally stubbled. His eyes were so blue they immediately reminded Charlotte of the vast sky outside—vivid and sharp. His mouth was disconcertingly sensual—a contrast to the hard angles of his body and bone structure.

A loose-fitting white shirt did little to disguise the solid mass of muscle on his chest and a tantalising glimpse of dark hair. It was tucked into very worn jodhpurs that clung to hard and well muscled thighs in a way that could only be described as provocative. Scuffed leather boots hugged his calves.

It was only then, belatedly, that Charlotte registered the very earthy and surprisingly sensual smell of horse-flesh and something else—male sweat. To her utter horror she realised that she was reacting to him as if she'd taken complete leave of her senses.

He frowned. 'Mrs McQuillan?'

She nodded, only vaguely registering that he'd got her title wrong.

'You were leaving?'

His deep and intriguingly accented voice reverberated through her nerve-endings in a very distracting way.

Charlotte finally broke herself out of the disturbing inertia that was rendering her insensible. What on earth was wrong with her? It wasn't as if she hadn't seen a handsome man before. She tried to ignore the fact that she'd just made such an intense inspection of the man and shelved her unfortunate reaction to him until she could study it in private, later.

She looked him in the eye. 'I've been waiting here for over an hour, Your Majesty, I thought you weren't coming.'

Those remarkable eyes flashed with what looked like censure. 'I'm not king yet.'

He looked down, and Charlotte became conscious of her rigid grasp on her case. She forced herself to relax.

He met her eye again. 'Were you offered any refreshment?'

Charlotte shook her head. King—no, *Sheikh* Al-Noury walked back to the doorway and shouted for someone. A young boy in a long tunic and turban appeared—the same one who had shown her into the office—looking pathetically eager to please. He looked terrified, however, after the stream of rapid Arabic Sheikh Al-Noury subjected him to, and then he ran.

When Charlotte registered what he'd said she stepped forward saying heatedly, 'That was uncalled for! How was he to know to offer me anything when he only looks about twelve? Someone senior should have been here to meet me. Where are your staff?'

Sheikh Al-Noury turned around slowly. He arched a brow and leant against the doorframe, crossing his arms. Totally nonchalant and unfazed by her outburst. 'You speak Arabic?'

Charlotte nodded jerkily. 'Among numerous other languages. But that's not the point—'

He straightened from the door. 'I'm sorry. I would have been here to meet you but I got delayed at the stables, taking delivery of a new thoroughbred—a present from Sheikh Nadim Al Saqr of Merkazad. He was skittish after the journey so it took a while to settle him.'

Sheikh Al-Noury had crossed the expanse of the Royal Office before Charlotte could get her thoughts in order. The fact that his apology hadn't sounded remotely sincere was something that got lost in a haze as she found herself once again momentarily mesmerised by his sheer athletic grace. He moved like no other man she'd ever seen—all coiled muscle and barely restrained sexual magnetism. It was an assault on her senses.

He looked over his shoulder from where he was pouring dark golden liquid into a bulbous glass. 'Can I get you anything?'

Charlotte's throat suddenly felt as dry as the surrounding desert and she said, 'Just water, please, if you have it.'

He came back towards her, holding out a glass of iced water, and once again Charlotte was struck by his sheer physicality. She reached for the glass and their fingers touched. A raw jolt of electricity shot up her arm, making her accept it jerkily. She immediately raised it to her mouth to give herself something to do, feeling as if she was floundering. She didn't like it.

Sheikh Al-Noury indicated the chair from which she'd only just picked up her bag, intending to leave.

'Please, take a seat, Mrs McQuillan.'

He walked around to the other side of his desk and sat down, lifting his feet carelessly onto the desk-top and crossing them at the ankle. Charlotte's eyes grew wide at this less than respectful pose, and she forgot his offer to take a seat. Right now all he was missing was a half-naked showgirl sitting in his lap.

He swirled the drink in his glass and took a sip before looking at her and raising a brow. 'I presume from the expression on your face that I'm about to get my first lesson in diplomacy and etiquette?'

Charlotte dragged her horrified gaze away from the very battered soles of his boots. There were dark stains that looked and smelt suspiciously like animal waste, and as her gaze clashed with that painfully blue one she said frigidly, 'It is generally considered an insult of varying proportions to expose the soles of your feet to a guest anywhere in the world.'

The man did nothing for a long moment, and then he just shrugged minutely. 'Well, we are in *this* part of the world now—and, believe me, we have far more inventive ways of insulting people. Nevertheless, I will endeavour to refrain from insulting my etiquette advisor.'

He lifted his legs, which only drew Charlotte's attention to his thighs again, and then they were hidden from view under his desk. She felt the strangest twist in her belly. Almost a pang of regret. It angered her to be behaving so oddly.

That anger made her say through gritted teeth, 'I am much more than an "etiquette advisor", Sheikh Al-Noury. I am an expert in international relations and diplomacy, with a master's degree in Middle Eastern

Relations. I speak seven languages and I've just completed a successful assignment with King Alix Saint Croix, ensuring his smooth transition back onto the world stage after regaining his throne...'

Charlotte stopped and took a breath, slightly aghast at how much had just tumbled from her mouth.

Sheikh Al-Noury barely moved a muscle from his louche pose as he said, 'Mrs McQuillan—'

'And it's not *Mrs* McQuillan,' Charlotte snapped, feeling as if she was fraying from the inside out while this man remained utterly nonchalant. 'It's *Miss*.'

The sheikh's bright gaze dropped down over her upper body and back up, making Charlotte feel hot all over and yet as if she'd suddenly been found wanting. He'd obviously come to some unflattering conclusion about her single status.

He looked at her and said, with an almost infinitesimal twitching at the corner of his sensual mouth, 'Quite. Forgive me for the error. I'm afraid I'd just assumed...' He sat up straighter then, and pointed to the chair on the other side of his desk. 'Please, sit down, Miss McQuillan. You're making me nervous, looming over me like that.'

Charlotte doubted anything would make this man remotely nervous, and to her disgust felt perilously close to wanting to stamp her foot and storm out. Did he have to make her feel like an admonishing parent? And why should that be pricking at her insides like a hot poker?

Charlotte's habitual cool head was irritatingly elusive. She'd never been so aware of herself. She knew that she presented a slightly conservative front, but in her business it was paramount to appear at all times elegant and refined. Giving no cause for possible offence or provocation.

She reluctantly did as he'd bade and sat down, aware of her skirt feeling tight and the top button of her shirt digging into her throat. Clothes that had never felt restrictive before, now felt shrink-wrapped to her body.

He put the glass down on the desk and said, 'Look, your credentials are not in doubt. King Alix of Isle Saint Croix rang me himself to sing your praises. But the fact is that I did not look for your expertise. My brother hired you in spite of my protests. I would have told you before not to bother coming, but I'm afraid I got caught up in ensuring my business concerns are attended to in my absence. However, I will be more than happy to ensure your return to the UK immediately, and of course you will receive full payment in recompense.'

This man's casual disregard for who and what she was made Charlotte's hackles rise. As did his arrogant assumption that she would be so easily dismissed.

She pointed out with faux sweetness, 'As it was your brother who hired me, then I'm afraid he is the only one who has the power to terminate this contract.'

Sheikh Al-Noury immediately scowled, but it only enhanced the wickedly beautiful symmetry of his features. His gaze narrowed on her and she stopped herself from fidgeting.

'Are you seriously telling me that you would prefer to stay here in this landlocked sandpit of a country, in a city that is routinely plunged into darkness when the archaic electricity infrastructure fails, rather than be at home amongst your first-world comforts enjoying all of the festivities of the season? My coronation is due to take place a couple of days before Christmas, Miss McQuillan, and if you stay I can't guarantee that you'll make it home in time. You might not be married, but I'm sure there's someone who is expecting your...company.'

It took Charlotte a few precious seconds to assimilate everything he was saying, but what caught at her gut was the way he'd hesitated over the word *company*, as if he'd had to find a diplomatic—*ha!*—way of suggesting that there might be someone waiting for her.

Next she registered his obvious disdain for his inherited kingdom—*this landlocked sandpit of a country*. True, there was something pitilessly unrelenting about the sea of sand on all sides of this ancient city, but Charlotte had felt a quickening of something deep in her soul—an urge to go out and explore, knowing from her research and studies of this region that it hid treasures not immediately apparent.

Collecting her wits, she said coolly, 'I'm not in the habit of reneging on agreements, Sheikh Al-Noury, and it would be unprofessional in the extreme for me to walk away at this early stage. As for your kind concern about my missing Christmas, I can assure you that I have no particular desire or need to return in time for the holiday. In fact, it suits me perfectly well to be here right now.'

Salim looked at the woman on the other side of his desk—more than a little taken aback. He was used to issuing an order, or, in this case a very polite suggestion—and having it obeyed. But she was not walking out of his office as he'd fully intended—who wouldn't take pay for nothing?—instead she was sitting opposite him as straight and upright as a haughty ballet dancer, staring at him with eyes the kind of green he'd only ever seen in Scotland, on one of those ethereally misty days. Distracting. Irritating.

She wasn't remotely his type, so why was he noticing her eyes? Salim preferred his women a lot more *deshabillée*, accessible and amenable. Everything about her, from her shining cap of neatly bobbed shoulder-length hair to her pristine dark grey suit and light grey blouse, screamed control and order—constraints Salim had rebelled against for so long now that he couldn't remember a time when he *hadn't* wanted to upset the status quo.

And yet…much to his irritation…he couldn't help noticing the fact that her surprisingly lush mouth was at odds with her cool demeanour, making him wonder what other lushness might be hiding under her oh-so-prim and neat exterior.

His gaze dropped to the bow at her throat and he imagined tugging on one silken length—would her whole shirt fall open? As he watched, the silky material moved more rapidly over her chest, as if she was breathing quickly, and when Salim glanced up again her cheeks had a slight telltale flush.

He was well inured to the signs of attraction in women, but it was patently evident that this woman didn't welcome it. Which was a total novelty.

When he caught her eye again he almost felt the blast of ice along with an accusatory light. She definitely didn't like being attracted to him.

This intrigued him more than he cared to admit—as did her assertion that she didn't mind missing Christmas. But he curbed the impulse to ask her why. He avoided asking women searching questions.

Salim cursed himself and shifted in his chair to ease the sudden constriction in his pants. To find himself reacting to a woman who desired him but looked at him as if he was a naughty schoolboy was galling.

He forced his body back under control and stood up. Her gaze lingered around his chest area for a moment before rising. She stood up too—hurriedly. He had a sense that she was usually more composed—if that was possible—than she was now and that thought gave him some perverse pleasure.

'You're determined to see out your contract, then?'

She nodded. 'Yes.'

'How long did my dear brother hire you for?'

'Until the coronation takes place. He said that if you require my services after that you can extend the contract yourself.'

Salim thought to himself that as he had no intention of staying in his role as king for long that would be highly unlikely, but he desisted from sharing that information with a complete stranger.

'As you wish,' he said. 'If you really want to stay in this sand-blown place—'

'Oh, but I think it's beautiful…' She stopped, her cheeks going pink. 'I mean, from what I've seen so far. It's run down, yes, but one can see the potential.'

Salim arched a brow and ignored the pulse in his blood seeing this small glimpse of something like passion. 'Can one?'

Her green eyes flashed. Once again Salim found himself a little mesmerised by the vivid emotions crossing her face. He couldn't remember meeting a woman so lacking in artifice. And then something in him hardened. Was he losing his mind? All women wanted something from him—even this one.

Maybe she just wanted the kudos of working for him—it would certainly elevate her professional standing to be the one who had wrangled Sheikh Salim Al-Noury into accepting his crown and toeing the line like a good little king.

He thought of something and folded his arms. 'Aren't you worried that by being associated with me you'll taint your reputation?'

She tipped up her chin. 'I am here to see that that doesn't happen, Sheikh Al-Noury, and I'm very good at my job.'

For a second he stood in stunned silence, and then he couldn't stop a smile—a genuine smile—from curving his mouth upwards. It had been so long since anyone had exhibited such confidence in front of him. And a lack of awe that was as refreshing as it was slightly insulting.

She frowned. 'If you're going to make fun of me—'

Salim shook his head. 'I wouldn't dare, Miss McQuillan. I'd be afraid you'd put me over your knee and spank me for being naughty.'

The colour deepened in her cheeks, as if she was having trouble controlling her temper and Salim *almost*, but not quite, regretted goading her like this.

But then she recovered and reached for her case. She avoided his eye. 'If that's all for now, Sheikh Al-Noury, I think I'd like to settle in and get acquainted with my surroundings.'

He put out a hand. 'By all means. Let me show you to your room.'

She preceded him out of the Royal Office. She was taller than he'd initially registered. The top of her head would come to just under his chin. Her body would stand tantalisingly flush against his in heels. But if she wasn't wearing heels... Once again sexual interest flared in his groin and he scowled. She was buttoned up to within an inch of her life. Since when had he found *prim* attractive?

Charlotte was burningly aware of Sheikh Al-Noury close behind her, and it made her tense—even though she knew that he wasn't remotely interested in her in that way. She was sure he didn't taunt women he found attractive and suggest they might put him over their knee, which had caused all manner of completely inappropriate images to flood her mind.

The man was so charismatic, he could probably make an inanimate object feel something.

He led her away from the office down a long, imposing corridor. She'd only seen a handful of staff so far, which added to the surreal sense of the whole palace being in a state of arrested development.

Salim glanced at her when she'd caught up with his long-legged stride and she said, 'I'm surprised the palace is so quiet. Is there only a skeleton staff because no one has been in residence for so long?'

Sheikh Al-Noury stopped, causing Charlotte to come to a halt too. 'There is minimal staff today because it's a national holiday—don't tell me you missed that in your research?'

She *had* missed that pertinent detail, and now she felt foolish after spouting off all her qualifications.

'Don't worry,' he drawled, striding off again, 'I'll make sure someone attends to you and brings you food. Tomorrow you'll be assigned a maid—'

'That's really not necessary,' Charlotte protested as she started after him. She was aware of the customs here, but wasn't comfortable at the thought of someone waiting on her.

'It's how things are done, Ms McQuillan,' the sheikh pointed out. 'If you insist on staying then you will abide by our ways.'

Charlotte stopped for a moment, surprised that in this he seemed to be happy that customs were adhered to, but she had to keep going when he showed no signs of slowing down and was about to disappear around a corner. She wouldn't put it past him to leave her lost in this vast palace. It couldn't be more obvious that he'd prefer to be putting her on the next flight home.

She longed to be able to stop and explore as they passed intriguing-looking courtyards with colourful mosaics and ornate fountains. They rounded another corner and Charlotte jumped when a peacock appeared in their path, as nonchalant as if they were intruding on its turf, its long and vibrantly coloured tail trailing behind it.

Sheikh Al-Noury stepped around it and kept going. Charlotte felt disorientated. She'd built a picture of this man in her mind that had been based on lurid headlines:

Playboy Sheikh opens new nightclub in Monte Carlo!

Al-Noury triples fortune overnight by floating new social media messaging site!

And, while he wasn't doing much to dispel that image with his appearance or attitude, he didn't seem as…shallow as Charlotte might have expected.

They came to a set of huge double doors at the end of the corridor. Sheikh Al-Noury opened them and stood back to let her precede him. When Charlotte stepped over the threshold she sucked in a breath. This was a different palace. One that hadn't been frozen in time and left to crumble to pieces.

It was a suite containing numerous rooms, each one covered in exquisite Persian carpets. The furnishings were sumptuous and sensual—dark reds and purples. A little over the top for her tastes, but effortlessly regal. There was a private dining area, and a living room that led into a palatial en-suite bedroom dominated by a four-poster bed.

She avoided looking at that, acutely aware of the man only feet away and how he might be observing her reaction and somehow judging her. She'd never felt so conscious of being a woman before. And a woman who was lacking.

The room was pleasantly cool, thanks to the air-conditioning, and there were floor-to-ceiling windows and French doors that led out onto a private terrace, complete with a decorative swimming pool.

She turned around to face her reluctant host. 'These rooms are beautiful, but I'd be quite happy in something less...luxurious.'

He waved a dismissive hand. 'These are usually reserved for my mother's use, and they were decorated to her specifications, but as she won't be visiting any time soon you are welcome to use them.'

There was a distinctly chilly tone to his voice and Charlotte said, 'Not even for your coronation?'

Sheikh Al-Noury's face became shuttered. 'She knows she's not welcome here while I'm in residence.'

Charlotte couldn't claim much of a relationship with either of her parents, but the cold tone of Sheikh Al-Noury's voice shocked her. 'But isn't this her homeland?'

He responded curtly. 'It was.'

He backed away then, and suddenly Charlotte had an irrational fear of being left alone in this seemingly empty palace. In truth, it wasn't a totally irrational fear because she'd had plenty of experience being left to her own devices, with only a nanny and staff for company in big houses, but she refused to think of her own demons now.

She'd already revealed too much by admitting she had no desire to be at home for Christmas. Not that he'd shown much interest in why that might be. Not that she wanted him to show interest she told herself fervently. So she said nothing.

He was almost at the door when he turned back and said, 'Please, make yourself comfortable. I'll instruct someone to bring you some dinner.'

So she was to be consigned to her rooms.

But then he added, 'Do feel free to explore... I must warn you, though, that it is perilously easy to get lost in this place, so don't stray too far. The palace library is on this corridor, if you go left when you step outside.'

Just before he disappeared Charlotte blurted out, 'Sheikh Al-Noury?'

He turned around, his hand on the door. 'Yes?'

For a moment her mind went dismayingly blank at the way he so effortlessly dominated even this vast room, but she forced herself to focus and said, 'I'm not here to be a nuisance... I am actually here to try and help ease your transition into becoming king.'

She could see his jaw clench from where she stood, and he said, 'Miss McQuillan, you wouldn't be here if it had been up to me. The last thing I need is an expert in diplomacy. But you are here, and I suspect you're going to prove to be a nuisance whether you intend to or not, so you can start by calling me Salim. The way you say Sheikh Al-Noury makes me feel old.'

Before Charlotte could respond to that, or object to the way he insisted on calling *her* Miss McQuillan, as if she were a headmistress, he said, 'I'll have someone bring you some food, and I suggest that in the meantime we stay out of each other's way.'

CHAPTER TWO

CHARLOTTE WATCHED THE door close on the most infuriating man she'd ever met, not to mention the most disturbing, and she had to quell a childish urge to hurl something at the door behind him. Instead she kicked off her shoes and paced back and forth on the sumptuous silken rugs.

She fumed. She was used to dealing with clients who thought they knew everything about international relations and diplomacy until something blew up in their faces, and then suddenly Charlotte became their most valuable asset. But she'd never encountered such downright…antipathy before.

She was patently unwelcome—and she could call him Salim but he wouldn't deign to call her Charlotte. She thought about that for a moment and felt a frisson run down her spine at the thought of his tongue wrapping itself around her name. That little frisson was humiliating, because it was glaringly obvious that he didn't view her as female—more as an asexual irritation.

Sheikh Al-Noury was affecting her in a way that she hadn't experienced before, because she was good at keeping people at a distance and yet from the first moment they'd met he'd slid under her skin with disconcerting ease.

Charlotte shucked off her jacket and undid the bow at her neck and her top button. Then, spying her bags in the bedroom near the dressing room, she set about unpacking. She found herself dwelling on the animosity the sheikh had demonstrated towards his mother. She didn't like the way it resonated within her, reminding her of her own fractured relationship with her mother, brought on by years of careless parenting after a bitter divorce.

But she diverted her mind away from wondering too much about anything personal to do with the sheikh. It wasn't her business. And the last thing she wanted to think about was her own pitiful family history.

After taking a refreshing shower in the lavish bathroom, Charlotte changed into stretchy pants and a soft long-sleeved top. Just as her stomach rumbled she heard a knock on the door. Her gut clenched as she imagined it might be him, but when she opened the door there was a young girl, with a trolley full of food and wine in an ice bucket on the other side.

She admonished herself; he'd hardly be delivering her dinner.

Charlotte stood back to let the girl in and watched as she silently laid the dining table for one and set out the food. Tantalising scents filled the air and her stomach rumbled louder. The girl scurried out again, too shy to return Charlotte's smile.

Charlotte sat down to explore what she'd been given. Balls of rice mixed with herbs. Lamb infused with spices and scented rice. Flat bread with hummus. It looked delicious and she found that she was ravenous.

She ate as dusk fell outside, not noticing it had got dark until she stood up and went to the window with her wine glass in her hand, feeling a little more settled after an unsettling day.

She opened the French doors and was surprised to find that it was much cooler than she'd expected—and then she chastised herself: basic geography, of course it got cold in the desert at night. She fetched a cashmere wrap and then went back outside, sitting on a seat, relishing the peace.

The thought of the vast expanse of empty desert surrounding her made a thrum of excitement pulse in her blood. She'd always found this part of the world fascinating, hence her choice of master's degree. The stars were so low and bright in the dark sky she imagined she could reach out and pluck one into her hand.

Tabat intrigued her.

And so does its enigmatic ruler, whispered a voice.

Charlotte scowled and took a sip of wine, telling herself that Sheikh Al-Noury—*Salim*—didn't intrigue her at all. He was thoroughly charmless and clearly reluctant to change his hedonistic existence before becoming king.

He didn't intrigue her because she knew his type all too well. As the only child of two high-profile parents, who had used her as an unwitting pawn in their bitter divorce and custody battle, she recognised the traits of a selfish person who was here under sufferance. After all, when her father had lost in the custody battle with her mother he'd always let it be known that her visits with him had been something he'd done purely out of legal obligation, not because he really cared for her, so she was in far too familiar territory.

However, she wouldn't let her own personal feelings intrude on her professional life. She'd worked too hard to separate herself from her parents and that time. She'd even changed her name, vowing to live a life much different from theirs, which was smack at the centre of the public eye.

She'd built an independent life and a reputation based on her intellect—not her name or the infamy associated with it. She had a strong desire never to be at the mercy of anyone else again, to the point that she'd instinctively avoided intimate relationships, too afraid of letting someone close enough to devastate her world as her parents had.

Diverting her mind away from her past, she assured herself that all she had to do was make sure the sheikh didn't cause an international scandal in the run-up to his coronation, which was due to take place in three weeks. And then, once the man had been crowned king, Charlotte could walk away and hopefully never see him again.

So why did she find her mind wandering back to him now? Wondering where he was in this vast and largely empty palace?

Then she cursed her naivety as a wave of embarrassment made her feel hot. He had surely not denied himself the pleasures of a mistress. A man like that? He'd left his life of excess in Europe and the States, to return to take up his rightful place, but he'd hardly have denied himself his base comforts, and sex and women were one of his most well-documented pastimes. And only the most beautiful women at that—albeit never for long.

Charlotte shook her head and stood up, returning to her suite. She told herself firmly that she couldn't care less if Sheikh Salim was entertaining a harem of mistresses right now as long as he was discreet about it.

The fact that it took her ages to fall asleep in the huge bed, only for her dreams to be populated by a mysteriously masked and robed man on a huge stallion cantering across vast desert sands, was a pure coincidence. And not disturbing in the slightest.

Not even when she had to concede when she woke the following morning that he hadn't really been mysterious at all. Not with those blue eyes.

A week later

'Sire, we are so grateful that you are here, finally. There is so much work to do in two weeks! And then, once you are king—'

Salim turned around abruptly from where he'd been trying to tune out his chief aide, stopping the man's words. They caused a sensation not unlike panic in his chest and Salim did not panic.

His aide—an old man who had known his grandfather—looked at him expectantly. Salim said tightly, 'Do whatever it is that you deem necessary, Rafa. You know more about this place than me, after all.'

The slightest flare of something in those old eyes was the only hint that his aide was not impressed that it had taken Salim so long to take up his role, or that he'd spent most of the last week out of Tabat.

Salim told himself that part of his motivation for leaving Tabat behind for a few days hadn't had anything to do with Charlotte McQuillan and her big green eyes looking at him so incisively. Not unlike the way Rafa was looking at him right now.

It had actually had to do with the secret meetings he'd set up with his legal team, and a close friend who ruled a nearby sultanate, to discuss who best to approach to take over from him as king once he'd abdicated.

The meetings hadn't gone well. The one person he

and his team had identified as a suitable prospective king had turned them down flat. A distant cousin of Salim's, Riad Arnaud.

The man was a billionaire and a respected businessman. He had ancestral links to this world and had inherited a tiny uninhabited Sheikhdom on the borders of Tabat and Jandor—a mining hub that workers commuted in and out of from nearby Jandor.

But, he was also a single father with a young daughter and he was adamant that he didn't want to turn his life upside down, thrusting her into a life of duty and service and taking her away from her home in France, where they lived.

Salim of all people had to respect his cousin's decision, after all, he knew the consequences of having choice taken away from you.

His friend Sultan Sadiq of Al-Omar had borne the brunt of Salim's frustration once his team had left.

When he'd finished extolling the potential virtues of Tabat that would be enjoyed by its next king his friend had just looked at him with an arched brow and asked mockingly, 'If it's such a hidden jewel then why are you so eager to pass it up?'

The fact that his friend's question had caused Salim to stop momentarily was not something he wanted to dwell on. Nor was the fact that it had made him recall Charlotte McQuillan's assessment that Tabat had potential. This was not his destiny and he would not be swayed.

In a bid to deflect his mind from that incident and from his conscience, which was proving to be dismayingly persistent, Salim asked, 'Miss McQuillan…where is she now?'

Rafa's eyes lit up. He was clearly anticipating that

Salim was finally ready to seek advice on becoming a good king. But Salim had far more carnal urges on his mind than discussions of diplomacy and he didn't like it. She wasn't his type.

Even with a vast desert between them he'd found the image of her green eyes staying with him, along with the provocative image of that damned silk bow tied so primly at her throat.

Rafa interrupted Salim's thoughts when he answered, 'She wanted to go sightseeing today, so I sent one of my junior assistants with her. They've gone to the *wadi* just outside the city limits.'

Salim frowned, his irritation increasing for no good reason. 'Which junior assistant went with her?'

Rafa looked nervous. 'Kdal, sire. He's one of my most trusted assistants—I assure you he'll take care of her.'

Picturing the young man's prettily handsome face and obsequious manner in his mind's eye, Salim found himself saying, 'Instruct the groom to get my horse ready.'

Charlotte was doing her best not to stand with her mouth hanging open, but it was hard in such a jaw-droppingly beautiful location. The *wadi* was just out-side Tabat City—a deep river valley carved out of the earth. A sheer high wall of rock was on one side, dotted with palm trees at the base. The other side was flat and verdant, and obviously a popular beauty spot, although it was quiet today.

Kdal, her attentive guide, had explained that this *wadi* was always full of water due to the underground streams. The water looked green and all too inviting in the blazing midday heat.

Kdal was now guiding her over to where a makeshift table had been set up, under a tent that offered some much needed shade.

'We're having lunch here?' she asked, charmed by the idea, and also by the delicious smells coming from where a small cluster of rustic buildings stood.

'Yes, Miss McQuillan. We thought you'd enjoy the view. This is a well-known spot for travellers to stop and seek refreshment. I hope you don't think it's too basic…'

Charlotte was about to respond *not at all* but then suddenly Kdal disappeared from her eyeline and Charlotte looked down to see him prostrated at her feet. She was about to bend down and see if he'd fainted when she heard a sound behind her, and turned to see a mythically huge black stallion on top of which sat a man with a turban covering his head and face. He wore a long robe.

It was so reminiscent of her dreams that Charlotte wondered if she was suffering from sunstroke—and then the man swung his leg over and stepped gracefully off the horse, which snorted and gave a shake of its massive head.

All Charlotte could see, though, was the bright flash of blue eyes. Far too familiar blue eyes. *Sheikh Al-Noury.* Her pulse tripped and galloped at double-time.

He pulled down the material covering his mouth and said with a glint in his eye, 'You don't look very enthusiastic to have me join you for lunch.'

It *was* him. She wasn't dreaming.

A man appeared, seemingly from out of thin air, to lead the sheikh's stallion away, and she saw a sleek blacked out four-by-four vehicle purring to a stop nearby, presumably carrying his security detail.

Charlotte called on all her skills to recover, and said

as equably as she could, 'Well, if you recall, you told me that you believed my presence would be a nuisance and that you intended for us to stay out of each other's way—hardly leading me to suspect that you'd seek out my company.'

He didn't look remotely repentant. He looked breathtakingly gorgeous as he lazily pulled the turban off his head. Dark hair curled wildly from where it had been confined under his turban, and his jaw was even more stubbled than she remembered. He was wearing the jodhpurs again, and the long tunic did little to disguise the sheer masculine power of his body.

Charlotte hated that she was wearing pretty much the same outfit she'd been wearing the first time she'd seen him.

As if reading her mind, his gaze slipped down from her face and he asked, 'Do you own a similar shirt in every colour of the rainbow, Miss McQuillan?'

Defensively Charlotte answered, 'No, actually. But I find that in my line of work it's prudent to be smartly dressed at all times, and I'm mindful of not offending anyone by wearing anything too casual or revealing.'

His eyes met hers, and she could have sworn his mouth twitched.

'No, that wouldn't do at all.'

He gestured to the table behind them, and when she turned she saw that it was now miraculously set for two, with gleaming silverware and sparkling glasses on a white tablecloth. Kdal had disappeared, the little traitor.

'Please sit, Miss McQuillan.'

She sat down, feeling on edge, cursing Kdal for not warning her to expect the sheikh, who sat down opposite her. Even though they were out in the open air it suddenly felt claustrophobic.

Muted sounds came from the direction of the small cluster of buildings. There was an air of urgency that hadn't been there a few minutes before. The sheikh had clearly injected the *wadi* staff with adrenalin.

He took a sip of water and said, 'I'm sure you've noticed a change in the palace since the first day you arrived.'

Charlotte looked at him and had to admit, 'It's like a different place.'

When she'd woken up on her first morning and gone for an exploratory walk the place had gone from being eerily empty to buzzing with activity.

She said, 'I didn't realise the national holiday was to commemorate the anniversary of your grandfather's death. I'm sorry.'

The sheikh shrugged. 'Don't be. I hardly knew him. He died when I was a teenager.'

'So there's been a caretaker government here since then, until your father passed away?'

He nodded, and just then a waiter materialised, dressed in a pristine white tunic. The sheikh issued a stream of Arabic too fast for Charlotte to understand, and when the waiter had left he turned back to her.

'I hope you don't mind—I've ordered a few local delicacies.'

Charlotte narrowed her eyes at him across the table, suspecting strongly that this man would ride roughshod over anyone who let him. 'Actually, I prefer to order for myself, but I'm not a fussy eater.'

He sat back, that twitch at the corner of his mouth more obvious now.

'Duly noted, Miss McQuillan. Tell me, is that a Scottish name?'

He threw her with his question, and Charlotte busied herself unfolding her napkin in a bid not to let him see how easily an innocent question like that rattled her. Because it wasn't the name she'd been born with. It was her maternal grandmother's name.

'I...yes. It's Scots-Irish.' And then, before he could ask her more questions, she said, 'I had a tour of the city this morning with Kdal. He was very informative.'

She stopped when she saw something flash across the sheikh's face but it was quickly replaced with a very urbane expression, and he said, 'Please, tell me your impressions—after all, you did say that you thought it had much potential.'

Charlotte looked at him suspiciously, thinking he was mocking her, but his expression appeared innocent. Well, as innocent as a sinfully gorgeous reprobate could look.

'Well, obviously it needs a lot of work to restore it, but I found it fascinating. I had no idea how far back some of the buildings date. The mosque is breathtaking, and I hadn't expected to see a cathedral too.'

Sheikh Al-Noury took a sip of the white wine that had been poured into their glasses. 'The city has always been a multi-faith society—one of the most liberal in the region. Outside the city limits, however, the country runs on more traditional tribal lines. Tabat used to run all the way to the sea. Jahor, the capital of Jandor, was merely a military fortress until its warriors rose up and rebelled, creating a separate independent state and endless years of war. Tabat is where all the ancient treasures reside. And all the knowledge. We have a library that rivalled the one at Alexandria, in Egypt, before it was destroyed.'

Another waiter arrived with an array of food as Charlotte responded dryly, 'Yes, I've spent some time in the library this week—it's very impressive.'

The sheikh—she still couldn't think of him as *Salim*—gestured to the food. 'Please, help yourself. We don't really have a starter course.'

Charlotte felt self-conscious as she picked a little from each plate and added it to her own. She had to admit that she loved the Tabat cuisine as she tried a special bread that was baked with minced lamb, onions and tomatoes. Halloumi cheese and honey was another staple she was becoming addicted to. At this rate she'd have nothing to show for her time here except added inches to her waistline.

She watched Sheikh Al-Noury covertly from under her lashes, but he caught her looking and she could feel heat climb into her cheeks.

'You're not drinking your wine?' he observed.

She shook her head. 'I prefer not to when I'm working.'

He picked up his glass and tipped it towards her. 'I commend your professionalism. I, however, feel no similar urge to maintain appearances.' He took a healthy sip.

Feeling emboldened by his seeming determination to goad her, she said, 'I heard you have been away for most of the week.'

He put his glass down and his gaze narrowed on her. 'Yes. I was invited to the Sultan of Al-Omar's annual party in B'harani. He's an old friend.'

An image immediately sprang into her mind of the sheikh surrounded by beautiful women, and when she replied her voice sounded unintentionally sharp. 'I've heard of them… His parties are renowned for being impossible to get into, and they dominate the gossip columns for weeks afterwards, but there are never any pictures.'

'Yes,' he said, almost wistfully. 'That was in the good old days. But it's all changed now that he's a married man with children.'

'You don't approve, Sheikh Al-Noury?' Charlotte asked with faux innocence, almost enjoying herself now.

Those blue eyes pierced right through her. 'I thought I told you to call me Salim. And my friend Sadiq can do as he pleases. Every man seems to fall sooner or later.'

Charlotte ignored the little dart of emotion that surprised her, at the thought of this man falling for someone. 'Won't you have to...*fall* too? You'll be expected to take a queen and produce heirs once you are crowned king.'

Salim surveyed the woman opposite him, in another of those tantalising silk shirts with the damned bow that had haunted his dreams. Maybe she did it on purpose—projected this buttoned-up secretary image specifically to appeal to a man's desire to see her come undone.

It irritated him intensely that not one of the many beautiful women at Sadiq's party had managed to snare his interest. His old carousing friend had slapped him on the back and joked that he was becoming jaded. And then Sadiq's very pretty wife had joined them and whispered something in her husband's ear that had made him look at her so explicitly that even Salim, who was pretty unshockable, had felt uncomfortable.

When they'd made pathetically flimsy excuses and left, he'd silently wished them well in their obvious happy domesticity, while repeating his own refrain that he would never be snared like that. Because to commit oneself to another person was to risk untold pain.

When he'd lost his sister the grief had been so acute that for a long time he'd wanted to die too. After he'd passed through that dark phase and emerged on the other side he'd never wanted to love anyone again. It was simply too devastating. Loss had eaten away at his soul until there had been nothing left but a need to escape from the world that had brought him such pain and avenge his sister's death—which he had done.

Not that it had brought him any peace.

Angry to find his thoughts straying down this path, Salim said tersely in response to her question, 'No, Miss McQuillan, I won't have to *fall.*'

He felt an overwhelming urge to unsettle this woman who looked so pristine. So in control. So...unaffected.

'Because,' he said carefully, 'I have no intention of being King of Tabat for any longer than absolutely necessary.'

Shock bloomed across her expressive face, exactly as he'd expected, but it failed to bring any measure of satisfaction and that irritated Salim intensely.

She sat up. 'What do you mean? You're being crowned in two weeks—of course you'll be king.'

'Not for long,' he said grimly, regretting having said anything.

She shook her head, the shining cap of strawberry-blonde hair distracting him for a moment. She was so pale against this exotic backdrop. He imagined his darkness against her pale perfection...

'What on earth are you talking about?'

Her cut-glass tones enflamed Salim's arousal instead of dousing it. Only his friend Sadiq and his legal team knew of his plans. He shouldn't have said anything to this woman, who was still a relative stranger...and yet he relished the easing of a weight off his shoulders.

'I'm going to abdicate and ensure that a far more suitable person takes over as king in my place.' Even if the signs of finding that person weren't very encouraging.

Salim was mesmerised by the play of emotions over her face and he realised that she was quite beautiful. More beautiful for not being showy or wearing layers of make-up. She was obviously struggling to understand. He almost felt sorry for her.

'But...if you're intent on abdicating then why be crowned in the first place?'

'Because the country isn't entirely stable at the moment. There are tribal factions who want to see the city restored to a conservatism that hasn't existed for years. They've been growing stronger. If I was to walk away now it would create a vacuum, which they would use as an opportunity to storm the city and take over...there is a real danger of warfare.'

She glanced around them before whispering forcefully, 'But if you abdicate won't the same thing happen?'

Salim shook his head. 'By the time I abdicate I will ensure that whoever takes my place will be a force for good in the country. Someone who will command the respect of everyone and see the country into the future.'

She looked unimpressed and sat back, shaking her head. 'Isn't that meant to be you? Why would you do this when it's *your* destiny?'

Salim put down his napkin on the table, his skin prickling for exposing himself like this. 'You call being bred with calculated precision destiny? If it *was* destiny then my twin sister would be queen—she was born ten minutes before me—but because she was a girl and therefore deemed unsuitable, I was named the heir to the throne of Tabat.'

She looked at him, her face pale. 'You have a sister? I didn't realise…'

He curled his hand into a fist on the table and forced himself not to look away from that too-direct green gaze. 'She's dead. A long time ago.'

Charlotte felt the sheikh's—*Salim's*—tension. It crackled between them.

'I'm sorry, I didn't know… There was no mention…'

She was still reeling from what he'd just revealed about his plans as king…or non-plans. And that he'd had a sister.

'How did she die?'

Salim looked at her for a long moment, but Charlotte had the sense he wasn't seeing her. Then his focus narrowed to her again and she shivered.

'It doesn't matter how she died. She did. It's in the past now.'

But Charlotte had a very keen sense that it wasn't in the past at all. To change the subject a little, she pointed out, 'Your brother seems happy to accept his role.'

Salim's hand tightened around his napkin. 'My brother and I are very different people. I made my life far away from here. I have numerous business concerns around the world… I employ thousands of people. Are they worth any less than the people of Tabat?'

'No, of course not…but surely there is a way to run your businesses while also ruling Tabat?'

He inclined his head and his mouth tipped up slightly, as if mocking her. Charlotte felt heat rise. He was obviously finding her naive or clueless.

'I'm sure if I wanted to I could find a way, Miss McQuillan, but the truth is that I'm not prepared to make that sacrifice. Tabat deserves a committed and devoted ruler. I am not that man.'

Why? The word almost fell out of Charlotte's mouth, but she clawed it back at the last moment.

Salim sat back then, and said, 'I'm hosting a party in the palace this weekend. You are, of course, more than welcome. If you're still here.'

If you're still here.

Charlotte schooled her features, not liking the dart of hurt she felt that he was still intent on getting rid of her. 'Do you think the prospect of one of your infamous parties is enough to scare me off?'

He arched a brow. Supremely comfortable. Supremely dangerous. '*Infamous*? Please, do tell me what you've heard. I'm intrigued.'

She cursed her runaway mouth. 'That they're a by-word in hedonism and last for days. The last party you hosted at an oasis in the Moroccan desert ended with several of the guests being airlifted to hospital.'

He shook his head. 'I hate to burst your righteously indignant bubble, Miss McQuillan, but contrary to what was reported the helicopter was for me, to take me to the airport in Marrakech so that I could make a meeting in Paris. Nothing more salacious than that. The party broke up a couple of days later of its own accord, and I can assure you that no one suffered anything more than sunburn and a hangover.'

Charlotte immediately felt like assuring him that she wasn't an avid follower of tabloid gossip and that she'd only read about it while researching him and Tabat, but she resisted. 'I told you, I've no intention of reneging on my contract.'

Salim shrugged and finished his wine. 'Suit yourself.'

Struggling to try and find some equilibrium again, some vague sense of being in control, Charlotte said,

'I really don't think that a similar party would go down well here—unless it's part of your plan to deliberately paint yourself in such a negative light that you think it'll make your abdication welcome.'

He considered her words for a long moment, and then said, 'Not a bad idea at all, Miss McQuillan. Are you sure you aren't in the PR field?'

Before she could answer he said, 'As much as your idea has some merit, I'm not as crass as that. The last thing I want is to portray Tabat in an unfavourable light. After all, I'm on a campaign to make it as desirable as possible. So, no, this party won't be featuring scenes of Bacchanalian debauchery, it'll be very civilised and elegant.'

Charlotte felt tight inside, and wasn't even sure where all this emotion was flowing from. 'So you're effectively advertising your kingdom to the highest bidder?'

His mouth tightened for a moment, before relaxing into its habitual sensual lines. 'Let's just say I'm taking an opportunity to showcase its allure and beauty.'

The waiter came then, and removed their plates.

When he'd left Salim sat forward and said, 'As I said, Miss McQuillan, you're more than welcome to join us. The dress code will be full evening dress.'

Charlotte could well imagine the haute couture finery at one of his parties and thought of her one very classic, but boring black evening-dress that would only reinforce whatever negative impression he'd already formed of her. She forced a fake smile. 'Unfortunately I don't have any such clothes with me. I'll have to decline your generous invitation.'

Salim stood up to leave. 'That's too bad, Miss McQuillan. I rather like the idea of seeing you dressed in something less...formal.'

That bright blue gaze dropped lazily down her body and back up again.

For a moment Charlotte couldn't breathe. A wave of heat scorched her from the inside out. And then humiliation swiftly doused the heat. Seeing her in a dress would have zero effect on him. He was mocking her. Toying with her.

She stood up unsteadily. He held out a hand to indicate that she should precede him, but when she went to move her foot slipped out of her shoe. The heel was stuck in the soft ground.

She let out a gasp and hopped on one foot, bending down to get her shoe, but before she could do so a large hand was plucking it up.

She looked at Salim, who was now straightening up and holding her very staid court shoe. It had never looked less sexy.

That burn was back inside her. Mortification mixing with awareness.

To Charlotte's shock he went down on one knee before her, and his expression was far too innocent when he looked up and said, 'Let's see if it fits, shall we?'

She was no Cinderella and he was not Prince Charming.

Her face was burning as she took a quick glance around the *wadi*. Thankfully there was no one to be seen. She looked down at Salim and hissed, 'I can put it on myself.'

He sighed. 'Miss McQuillan, I have no doubt you can put on your own shoe, but I am offering to do it for you—and, believe me, I don't make a habit of helping women dress. It's usually the reverse, so this is a novelty. Humour me.'

She would have happily strangled him right then. She

put her foot out reluctantly and waited. She tensed herself, not even sure what she was tensing herself against, and when he cupped her heel in his other hand she wobbled precariously.

Because his touch will destroy you, a small voice said.

He looked up at her and his eyes seemed to have darkened, but she told herself it was her imagination. Feeling ridiculous and exposed, she tried to pull her foot away but his hold tightened. He slowly let her heel slide into the shoe, and to Charlotte's eternal embarrassment it was the single most erotic thing she'd ever experienced. Electric tingles went all the way up her bare legs, straight to her groin. Her nipples tightened.

Just when she thought she would be free he didn't let her go. His hand was warm on her calf, and for a crazy moment Charlotte imagined it travelling up her leg to the back of her thigh, where— She abruptly pulled her foot free of Salim's hands—successfully this time—horrified at where her mind had gone. She stood back and watched as he rose fluidly to his full height.

It must be second nature for him to toy with women as if they were playthings. And none better than her—gauche, and as far from his usual women as could be possible.

'Thank you,' she said tightly. 'But it was completely unnecessary.' She picked up her bag, avoiding his eye, and made her way out from under the shade of the tented structure. Staff appeared, bowing to their future king.

Little did they know, Charlotte thought to herself.

The man who had taken the horse away reappeared now, leading the huge animal. Instinctively Charlotte moved away—but then she felt a hand on her lower back and stopped dead. Salim was beside her, wicked devilry dancing in his eyes.

'I could offer you a ride back to the palace, if you like? It's a beautiful way to see the country.'

Charlotte imagined sitting in front of him on this horse, with his hand splayed across her belly, her bottom tucked far too close between his legs, and a tsunami of fresh awareness sizzled through her body.

She moved aside jerkily, out of his reach. 'No, thank you. I'm sure Kdal isn't far away, and he will take me back.'

'As you wish, Miss McQuillan. If you change your mind about the party do let me know. I'm sure we can find something suitable for you to wear.'

Inexplicably—because right then Charlotte was telling herself that one of his parties was the last place she'd ever want to be seen—she found herself yearning to be the kind of woman who could walk into a crowded room and have this man stop in his tracks because he was so captivated by her...

She cursed herself. What was wrong with her today?

Salim did something with the stirrups on his horse, adjusting them, and then with enviably athletic ease vaulted onto the horse's back. He wound the turban back onto his head, covering all that dark hair, and just before he pulled a piece back over his mouth he said, 'See you soon, Miss McQuillan.'

And then, with a flash of those blue eyes that seared right into her, he and the horse turned in one graceful fluid motion and he was gone, leaving nothing behind but swirling dust. Just to add to Charlotte's general feeling of dishevelment and inadequacy.

It got worse when she found her way to the small but functional toilet behind the catering area and looked at herself in the cracked mirror. She groaned out loud. Her hair was frizzy from the humidity and her nose was suspiciously red.

She'd just sat through lunch with that man looking like a scarecrow. A sun-burned scarecrow.

Damn him anyway.

CHAPTER THREE

'CASSIDY IS FAR too beautiful for you, my friend.' But even as Salim said the words they rang hollow. Even though they were true.

His cousin's lover stood a few feet away, talking to a small group. She was tall and striking, with dark red hair piled high on her head. A black sheath of a dress set off her pale skin and thoroughbred curves. She was one of the world's most sought after supermodels.

Riad Arnaud, who Salim had invited to the party in a somewhat futile attempt to entice his friend to reconsider his decision regarding becoming king, responded with a distinct bite to his voice, 'She's not available.'

Salim turned to the other man, who was dressed in a classic black tuxedo, as he was, and whistled softly. 'It's not like you to be possessive. Maybe there's another reason you don't relish the thought of leaving your life in France behind to become a king. Is she different, then? Are you going to succumb to a life of domesticity, like my brother and everyone else we know?'

He couldn't quite keep his voice as light as he'd intended.

Riad made a snorting sound. 'I've paid my domestic penance, as you well know, and the only good thing to come out of that situation was my beautiful daughter.

She's all I need. I will never let another woman close enough to cause havoc in my life again—they can't be trusted.'

They both heard a small sound and turned to see Riad's lover, Cassidy, with her hand to her mouth. Clearly she'd heard everything. Her eyes were huge and very blue. She turned abruptly and walked away.

Riad cursed colourfully and Salim watched him stride after his mistress. Salim shook his head at his cousin's folly—clearly the man was more involved than he wanted to admit.

Something twisted in his gut as he took in the ceremonial ballroom where he would be crowned in two weeks. The scene before him was a glittering, sumptuous exercise in promoting Tabat as a desirable kingdom.

His staff had worked tirelessly to bring the palace up to a standard it hadn't seen in a long time. Rafa had been so pleased and excited, seeing it as proof that Salim was about to turn the country's fortunes around.

The twisting in Salim's gut intensified as his conscience bit hard and a pair of familiar green eyes came into his mind. Eyes that he couldn't get *out* of his mind.

He turned around, irritation and frustration making his skin prickle. Would she turn up? Would she wear the dress he'd sent to her room after he'd heard nothing from her?

The prickling intensified and he looked towards the main door just in time to see her arrive. As if he'd conjured her up with his sheer will to see her.

Adrenaline surged in his blood as his far too avid gaze swept her from head to toe. And, even though she'd defied him, he couldn't stop the smile curling his mouth upwards or the raging heat in his body as he stalked to where she stood, willing that green gaze that had been haunting him to meet his...

Charlotte stood inside the main door to the ballroom and instantly felt like an utter fool. *She should have put on the dress.*

The dress that had been delivered to her room earlier that day. The most exquisite dress she'd ever seen. Green silk...strapless.

She'd held it up and the material had dropped to the floor with a whisper of expensive fabric. She had imagined how it would mould to her body. Emphasising curves she didn't even have and hiding any flaws and imperfections.

She had imagined how she would feel... As if she was the kind of woman who could walk into a room and have men look at her. Desire her.

One man in particular.

As that thought had entered her head she'd let the dress fall back onto the bed, aghast at how instantly it had seduced her. Seduced her into thinking for a second that she could risk the almost certain rejection she'd face.

Sheikh Salim Al-Noury had sent her this dress to toy with her. To mock her for staying and not leaving. If she put on the dress and went to his party, no matter how ironically she did it, she would be exposing herself in a way that would make her unbearably vulnerable.

Since her father had walked away from her all those years ago, effectively cutting himself out of her life, Charlotte had shunned intimate male attention and relationships. She was too fearful of experiencing that excoriating pain again. She knew it was irrational, and that no man could hurt her unless she allowed him to, but no man had slid under her skin so immediately and effectively as this reluctant king.

So, galvanised by hurt and anger that he thought he could manipulate her so easily for his own amusement, Charlotte had stormed off to find the party. She'd collided briefly in the corridor with a tall, arrestingly handsome man who'd looked vaguely familiar, even though she was sure she'd never seen him before, but that hadn't stopped her.

And now she was here and she felt like an impetuous idiot.

She'd never seen such a glittering scene. She wasn't sure what she had expected, but it was not this restrained...elegance. Candles bathed the guests in golden light. Men were dressed in tuxedoes. Women were arrayed in stunning jewel-coloured dresses with diamonds sparkling at their throats and hands.

A string quartet played on a dais in one corner. French doors were open to a long terrace, where more people mingled, and the dusk painted the vast sky outside purple and grey.

She was used to exclusive events, but always in a peripheral sense, because she was usually working. And she'd never felt more peripheral than right now, in her very boring skirt and shirt, with her hair pulled back in a tidy bun. She looked as if she was about to take dictation.

If Salim saw her now... She flushed with self-conscious heat to think of how he'd mock her—she'd have been damned if she'd worn the dress and was damned now that she hadn't.

She was about to turn to make her escape when she saw him, cutting a swathe through the crowd and coming straight for her, his eyes locked on hers. Intense.

Too late.

Even from here she could see the glint in his eye. The faintly turned up corner of that wicked mouth. It made a total mockery of her fantasy. He'd noticed her now for all the wrong reasons.

Her heart thumped and her skin grew clammy when he came to a stop in front of her. He was breathtakingly handsome. The tuxedo moulded to his muscles and tall frame like a second skin. It lent him an air of civility that had never felt more like a token gesture. His hair was still unruly and his jaw dark with stubble. This man was wild, through and through. As wild as the desert outside.

He drawled, 'Miss McQuillan—welcome. I shouldn't be surprised that you have chosen not to wear the dress; for someone whose career is all about diplomacy you've got a surprisingly rebellious streak.'

His words landed like tiny poisonous darts. Charlotte had never felt remotely rebellious before meeting him. She refused to be made so acutely aware of how she stood out like a limp flower next to hothouse orchids.

She curled her hands into fists at her sides. 'Believe me, you bring out my worst traits. Thank you for the dress, but it wasn't necessary. I'm not here for your amusement, I'm here to do a job, and that is to help you transition from your current role to your new one, no matter how long you choose to stay in it.'

He folded his arms across that massive chest. 'Haven't you heard that all work and no play makes Miss McQuillan a very boring girl?'

Charlotte sucked in air to try and calm her racing pulse and emotions. This man shouldn't be appealing to her emotions. But he was. And that was bad. It made her feel threatened and she blurted out words before she could stop herself or think them through.

'You know,' she said, 'maybe you're right. Maybe I should just call your brother and tell him that he's wasting his money.'

She'd turned to walk away, but before she could move a hard hand clamped around her wrist. Her pulse hammered against his hand. She looked at him, recalling all too easily how his hands had felt on her the other day.

Any mockery was gone from his expression now. 'You disappoint me…admitting defeat so easily?'

Before Charlotte could say a word her eye was caught by a stunning amazon of a woman dressed in a very revealing black lace dress. She was bearing down on them with a determined look on her vaguely familiar face. At the last second Charlotte realised she was a famous actress.

Salim had looked around too, but instead of letting Charlotte go his grip tightened and he muttered something rude under his breath, quickly turning and walking away, dragging Charlotte with him.

He'd taken her into an anteroom nearby and locked the door behind him before she'd even fully registered what had happened.

He stood with his back against the door and Charlotte looked at him. The air between them was suddenly charged with electricity. She was barely aware that the room was dark and opulently furnished, with books on every wall. Some kind of private sitting room or study.

Salim looked away from her and said, 'This was my grandfather's European room. He fancied himself in part as an English gentleman.'

Charlotte dragged her gaze from the man in front of her and took in the room properly. The gleaming mahogany desk with a reading lamp. The high-backed leather chair. The tartan carpet. The massive stone fireplace, which was completely incongruous when the desert lay beyond these walls.

'He always kept it to a colder temperature in here, so that he could pretend he was in England, or Scotland, and not the Middle East.'

It might be colder, but Charlotte felt hot. Her blood was sluggish in her veins, and yet she was jittery. A disturbing mix.

She looked back at the sheikh, saying unthinkingly, 'Salim…why have we come in—?'

But he interrupted her with a triumphant, *'Finally.* I knew I'd like the way you say my name.'

He started coming closer again and she shook her head, feeling as if she was losing her grip on reality. 'I don't…don't say it any differently from anyone else's name.'

He stopped in front of her. Too close. She took a step back.

'Ah, but you do, Miss McQuillan. You say it with that slightly frosty tone that tells me I'm not behaving as I should.'

She immediately felt defensive. 'I have a name too—it's Charlotte.'

She wasn't even aware that she was still backing away until she hit a solid surface. Shelves. She was breathing as if she'd just run a mile. All she could see were those blue eyes, boring into her.

Why was he looking at her like this? Making her blood leap and her skin prickle? Making her think of illicit things?

He stopped and put a hand over her head. Their bodies were so close they were almost touching. Charlotte felt threatened, but not by him. The threat came from the thought of her reaction to him…

And then he said it. '*Charlotte.*' And something she'd been clinging on to gave way inside her like a wall crumbling.

Desperately she said, 'You really should return to your guests—they'll be wondering where you are.'

He dismissed that with a quirk of his mouth. 'They'll survive.'

Charlotte reacted to his louche arrogance and to the insidious suspicion that even now he was just toying with her for his own amusement.

'Will they? Just like the people of Tabat will *survive* once you walk away from them?'

The intensity in the air around them changed immediately, becoming even more charged.

Salim's body was full of tension, his eyes hard. 'What do you care about Tabat and its people? You've only been here a week.'

Charlotte cursed herself for reacting to him. For exposing herself. 'I know I've only been here a week, but even in that time I can see that this is a great country and that the people deserve better.'

Salim's eyes were burning now, and his mouth was a hard line. 'Can you, now?'

Challenging him like this was heady in the extreme. All her life Charlotte had lived with the repercussions of being forced to choose one parent over the other in a bid to keep the peace—something that had inevitably had disastrous consequences. She'd built a life and a career out of keeping the peace. And yet now, here, with this man, something was breaking apart inside her...something incredibly freeing.

All she could see was that he was no better than her feckless parents, who had used her as an unwitting pawn. He was using her for his own entertainment.

Riling her up. Making her imagine all sort of crazy things…making her want things. *Him.*

She looked Salim straight in the eye. 'Life is so easy for you, isn't it? No wonder you don't want to rule—it would put a serious cramp in your lifestyle and a dent in your empire. Have you *ever* had to think of anyone but yourself, Salim? Have you ever had to consider the consequences of your actions? People like you make me—'

'Enough.' Salim punctuated the harshly spoken word by taking her arms in his hands. He said it again. 'Enough, Charlotte. You've made your point.'

She couldn't breathe after the way he'd just said her name. Roughly. His hands were huge on her arms, and firm but not painful. She knew she should say *Let me go* but somehow the words wouldn't form in her mouth.

Salim's eyes were blazing down into hers and for a second she had the impression that she'd somehow… hurt him. But in the next instant any coherent thought fled, because he slammed his mouth down onto hers and all she was aware of was shocking heat, strength, and a surge of need such as she'd never experienced before.

Salim couldn't recall when he'd felt angrier—people had thrown all sorts of insults at him for years. Women who'd expected more than he'd been prepared to give. Business adversaries he'd bested. His brother. His parents. But for some reason this buttoned-up slender woman with her cool judgmental attitude was getting to him like no one else ever had.

The urge to kiss her had been born out of that anger and a need to stop her words, but also because he'd felt a hot throb of desire that had eluded him for so long he'd almost forgotten what it felt like.

Her mouth was soft and pliant under his, but on some

dim level not clouded red with lust and anger he knew it was shock—and, sure enough, after a couple of seconds he felt her tense and her mouth tighten against his.

He knew he should draw back.

If he was another man he might try to convince himself he'd only intended the kiss to be a display of power, but Salim had never drawn back from admitting his full failings. And he couldn't pull back—not if a thousand horses were tied to his body. Because he wanted her.

He'd never tasted anything as sweet or felt anything as soft and enticing as her slender form. As if his harder edges had finally found their perfect match in spite of her tension.

Salim took his hands off her arms and wrapped them around her back, pulling her closer. He moved his mouth on hers without releasing her, coaxing a response. The proximity of their bodies would leave her in no doubt as to how he felt. His rock-hard erection was pressed against her soft belly and he could feel the thrust of her breasts against his chest.

He brought up a hand and cupped her jaw, angling her face up to his, and nipped gently at her lower lip. It felt soft, cushiony and yet firm. That message went straight to his erection, making it even harder.

Time was suspended for a long moment. This was a novelty for Salim, who found his lovers were usually so eager that they had laid themselves bare for his delectation before he'd even tried to take their clothes off.

Charlotte quivered like a bow in his arms, taut and delicate, and yet with a steely strength that made his blood roar. Salim used every skill in his arsenal to seduce her. He caressed the line of her jaw and cupped the back of her head, fingers tangling in her silky hair, making it come loose from its tidy bun.

He soothed her lip where he'd just nipped her and then he felt it…like a sigh moving through her body. The tension melted and her mouth softened under his.

The sense of triumph Salim felt might have shocked him if he'd been able to analyse it. But he was too busy capitalising on this moment, and on the tiny sliver of opportunity that came when her mouth opened minutely and Salim could coax it open further so that he could taste her sweetness fully.

When his tongue touched hers an electric current shot through his blood. His arm tightened around her even more, so that she was on tiptoe, the full length of her body flush against his, thigh to thigh, chest to chest. Breathing quickened as their fused mouths tasted and drank from each other. Charlotte's arms crept up around Salim's neck and she mimicked his moves.

He had an impression of shyness, and it was mind-bendingly erotic when he was used to women who thought being aggressive equated to being sexy.

Fuelled by a rising fever, Salim moved his hand down between their bodies and cupped Charlotte's breast through the slippery material of her silk shirt. It was fuller than he'd imagined, and that sent another electric frisson straight to his groin. She gasped into his mouth and went still. He could feel the bud of her hard nipple and pinched it lightly between his fingers, drawing back for a moment, finally taking his mouth from hers.

He felt drunk. Dizzy. Her lashes were long and dark against her flushed cheeks and she was biting her lips. They were moist and swollen.

'Look at me, Charlotte.'

Her name rolled off his tongue as if he'd been saying it all his life. He could recognise now that he'd been using *Miss McQuillan* to keep her at a distance. There would be no more distance, he vowed now.

It seemed to take an age for her to open her eyes, and when she did they were dark green, like Scottish moss after a rain shower. She looked as dazed as he felt.

Without taking his gaze off hers he let his fingers find the buttons on her shirt and he started to undo them, slipping them through the holes with gratifying ease, the silky material providing no resistance.

When her shirt was open to just below her breasts Salim looked down, and the breath hissed through his teeth at the provocative sight of the voluptuous bounty. Pale swells rising from dark grey lace.

He moved her shirt aside and, feeling rough and uncouth, tugged one lace cup down. Her breast popped free, revealing the sharp point of a pink nipple.

Salim's mouth watered. He'd never felt so turned on after little more than heavy petting. He cupped her breast and flicked his thumb back and forth across her nipple, seeing how it tightened even more, the aureole beading around it.

He looked at her. 'You like that?'

Charlotte's hands were gripping his arms and the need on her face was stark enough to render words superfluous. She looked stunned.

'I've wanted to see you like this,' he heard himself say hoarsely, 'undone...since the moment I walked into my office and found you waiting like a stern headmistress. All buttoned up and disapproving.'

Unable to resist tasting her again, he closed his hand around her breast. Her nipple stabbed his palm and he claimed her mouth again...greedy, desperate...and she opened up under him like a flower, arching her body into his and pushing her breast deeper into his palm.

Salim was oblivious to everything but the raging need in his body to embed himself deep in her silky heat until finally, *finally*, he might feel a sense of peace that had eluded him for as long as he could remember.

Charlotte had had the briefest moment of sanity when she'd tried her best to resist Salim after he'd started kissing her, but her resistance and that moment of sanity had been pathetically weak and illusory.

From the moment his mouth had touched hers it had been as if he'd reached inside her and lit a fire that was only his to light. A fire she'd hadn't even known could exist, consuming her to the point that all rational thought was burnt away.

This is what desire feels like...whispered a voice.

No one had ever made her feel like this before. She'd been on dates, she'd kissed men, but she'd always felt unmoved. As if she was standing outside herself and watching. It had reinforced her belief that keeping her distance was a good thing.

But right here, right now, with this man...distance was the last thing she wanted. She was fully in her body for the first time, and the sensations were so acute that it was almost painful.

Salim's tongue stroked hers with a sure mastery that she could only follow, and mimic blindly. His hand gripped her breast hard, but she wanted it even harder. She wanted him to pinch her nipple again, inducing that sting of shock followed by intense pleasure.

The fact that there was a room full of strangers just feet beyond where they stood, suspended in time, was something Charlotte was only very dimly aware of. The fact that she hated everything this man represented had also receded to some shadowy place she'd weakly turned her mind from.

The stubble of Salim's short beard scratched at her jaw as his mouth trailed from the corner of her mouth and down. Even that was erotic, sending shockwaves down deep into her core. Her head fell back, too heavy, and he pressed a hot open-mouthed kiss to her neck. She felt the sting of teeth and then his tongue, soothing. She was being held up only by his arm and the wall of shelves behind her.

It took a few moments for a rhythmic noise to break through the fog in her brain. She thought it was her heartbeat, but it wasn't, and when it registered properly she froze.

Someone was knocking on the door and she heard a panicky voice, 'Sire...? *Sire*...are you in there? Please?'

The door handle rattled and Salim's head came up. His hair was mussed and his eyes were heavy-lidded. His cheeks were flushed. He looked exactly how she imagined a fallen angel would look. Wicked and sexy and innocent all at once.

But as reality seeped back a chill wind skated over Charlotte's skin. She looked down to see her blouse hanging open and one breast bared, her nipple pink and hard. There were marks on her pale skin—marks from his fingers.

Mortification drenched her as the full enormity of what had just happened sank in.

Salim finally stepped back and jerkily she pulled up her bra.

She could still feel the press of his arousal against her belly, long and hard. It was small comfort, though, to know he'd been as turned on as her...it only made her feel even more confused.

She sent up silent thanks that her hands weren't shaking as she did up her shirt buttons. The lace of her bra chafed against her sensitised nipples and the betraying damp heat between her legs told of just how seismic this man's effect on her had been.

Charlotte risked a look at Salim. His mouth was open, as if he was about to say something, but just then the doorknob rattled again and Charlotte had never felt so relieved. She did not want to discuss what had just happened. Not when she felt so raw.

The panicked-sounding voice floated through. 'Please, *sire*…'

Salim was still looking at her, and Charlotte said with rising panic, 'Shouldn't you see who that is?'

Finally Salim issued an Arabic curse under his breath and turned around and strode to the door, his movements lacking their customary grace.

When he opened the door she heard Rafa's anxious voice say, 'Sire, there is something of utmost importance I need to tell you.'

Charlotte walked over to the door on wobbly legs, and when Rafa saw her his eyes widened, telling her in no uncertain terms that she wore the marks of Salim's lovemaking like a gauche teenager. Mortified all over again, Charlotte used the opportunity to escape, sliding around Salim, careful not to come into contact with him or meet his eyes.

She muttered something incomprehensible, and didn't look left or right as she left the revellers in the ballroom behind her.

When Charlotte reached the sanctuary of her rooms, she went straight into the bathroom and looked at herself in the mirror—and gasped. It was worse than she'd thought.

Her eyes were huge and dark green. Her lips were swollen. Her cheeks were flushed and her jaw was pink from Salim's stubble. Where her jaw met her neck there was a distinctive mark and she touched it now, remembering the nipping of teeth, the soothing of a tongue. His tongue.

With trembling hands she undid her shirt again and opened it, pulling down her bra to look at her breast. The marks of his hand were still on her pale flesh, but fading. Between her legs a pulse throbbed when she thought of the firm pressure of his hand on her flesh, her nipple trapped between two fingers.

She looked back at herself and almost didn't recognise the person reflected in the mirror. This was so far removed from the sane responsible person she thought she was—not given to whims or vagaries. Or spontaneous combustion.

Her legs were still dangerously wobbly and she put her hands on the sink in order to stay upright. She had memories of seeing her parents kissing, before they'd divorced, and they had always frightened her because there had been something so animalistic about it. But when she thought of how she'd behaved just now she realised that their impulses were hers too, in spite of everything. Genes will out, no matter what.

And yet how he'd made her feel for those few moments had been the most exciting thing that had ever happened to her.

Her fingers were curled so tight around the rim of the sink that she had to uncurl them for fear of cracking the porcelain.

There was a peremptory knock on her door and immediately she felt ridiculous, mooning at herself in the mirror. She did up her shirt and tried to smooth her hair, hoping the mark on her neck wasn't too visible.

Assuming it would probably be the nice girl who was

her obligatory maid—Assa—she opened the door to find her eye level not on the face of a pretty dark-eyed girl but on a very broad chest. A very familiar chest. A chest that not long ago she'd been rubbing her breasts against like a hungry little kitten.

She looked up to see Salim, his expression stern. Immediately she asked, 'What is it?'

'May I come in?'

Charlotte would have bet money on the fact that Salim was regretting what had just happened even more than her, so she stood back and tried not to notice how her body immediately hummed in close proximity to his again.

As he walked into the room she noticed that he'd lost his jacket and bow-tie. The top button of his shirt was open. He turned around to face her while she stayed close to the door, feeling like a coward.

Charlotte desperately wanted to say something before he had a chance to let her know how much he regretted what had to be a momentary lapse in judgement.

'What happened just now…it shouldn't have. It wasn't appropriate.'

Something flickered in Salim's piercing eyes, but it was gone before she could figure out what it meant. Probably relief that she wasn't making the most of an opportunity to embed herself in his life.

But then he said, 'Is that your professional opinion?'

Charlotte swallowed. 'Personal. And professional.'
Liar.

Salim raked a hand through his hair, making it even messier. 'We'll discuss that another time, but there are more important matters to deal with first.'

Charlotte's heart flipped over at the fact that he wasn't immediately agreeing with her about the kiss, and then she registered what else he'd said. 'What matters?'

Salim's mouth firmed. 'The reason Rafa was looking for me is because he's been informed that some of the bigger tribes are planning on marching into Tabat City in a bid to assert their dominance over each other before I am crowned king. They seek to curry favour, hoping for preferential treatment once I'm in power.'

Charlotte watched Salim pace back and forth, her gaze drawn helplessly to the fluid athletic grace of his body. She struggled to keep her eyes up.

She said quietly, 'They've been waiting for a long time for a leader. Without someone to unite and guide them any rifts and grievances between the tribes will have grown bigger and more entrenched.'

'Yes.' He stopped pacing and looked at her. 'So what I have to do is go and meet them before they can come to me—do my best to unite them and inform them that there will be no preferential treatment.'

At first Charlotte thought this was the most selfless thing she'd heard him say to date, but then she thought it through. 'But when you abdicate they'll doubt any assurances you've given them.'

Salim's mouth tightened. 'I'm meeting them all separately, and then I'll invite each tribal leader to the city to negotiate an agreement before the coronation. They'll be bound by that no matter what happens. A tribe's word is very important in this country.'

Charlotte cursed herself for being naive. He wasn't doing this because he cared about his people. Clearly this was all merely a means to an end—to make sure his own agenda succeeded. His agenda to pursue a life of independence and freedom, amassing more wealth than any one person could possibly know what to do with.

She said coolly, 'Well, as you've made it very clear that I'm of no use to you, I fail to see why you're telling me about your plans.'

Salim's face was carefully expressionless. 'The last thing I want to do is stir up any trouble while I'm visiting the tribes by unwittingly insulting anyone, so it looks as if I'll have need of your expertise after all—if you'll accompany me.'

Charlotte felt no sense of triumph at this *volte face*, only a rising panic at the thought of going anywhere with him. And yet how could she refuse when this was her reason for being there?

'Very well. I'll come with you.'

His expression was inscrutable. No more teasing or mocking. She wasn't sure how to deal with this far more serious Salim.

He nodded briefly in acknowledgement of her acquiescence. 'We'll leave tomorrow morning—early—and travel to the three main tribes over the next week.'

His gaze swept her up and down then, and she had to stop herself from folding her arms defensively, hoping she'd buttoned her shirt all the way up.

'Where we're going is a lot more traditional than the city, so I'll have Assa ensure you have the right clothes.' His blue gaze seemed to pierce right through her. 'It'll be very rustic, if you think you can handle that.'

Charlotte bristled at the tone in his voice, which cast doubt on her ability to endure a trip into the wild desert regions.

'Of course I can handle it. I've travelled extensively, and in my experience nomadic tribes often offer better hospitality than some five-star hotels.'

For the first time she thought she saw a flash of humour in his eyes, but he just said, 'Good. I won't have to worry that you'll run screaming from using an outdoor latrine, then.'

'No,' Charlotte said tightly, perversely liking the fact that she was so obviously nothing like the women he was used to and yet also irritated by it.

A moment stretched between them, and then Salim moved, walking towards her, back to the door. Charlotte stepped out of his way, her whole body tingling as he got close.

He had his hand on the knob when he looked at her again. 'About what happened…'

She looked at him and wished she had something to hold on to. She held on to her words. 'I told you—it shouldn't have happened.'

'And yet it did, and we both enjoyed it. And if you know anything about me by now, Charlotte, it's that I'm not in the habit of denying myself things that make me feel good.'

He'd turned and walked out before Charlotte could come back with some pithy response.

She tried to drum up some sense of outrage at his arrogance, but how could she when only minutes ago she'd been opening up underneath his touch like a flower unfurling for the sun?

She turned from the door and ignored the vivid splash of green silk on the bed in her peripheral vision, reminding her of the man's ability to get to her. She assured herself that his interest in her was fleeting, at best, and that once they went into the desert she would there in a professional role, on much firmer ground.

She kept assuring herself of this as she finally fell into a fitful sleep that night, beset by dreams of ominous shifting sands.

CHAPTER FOUR

'*IT SHOULDN'T HAVE HAPPENED.*' Salim waited impatiently for Charlotte to appear the following morning as dawn broke over Tabat. Her words, delivered in those cut-glass tones, still reverberated in his head. Irritating him intensely.

He was not used to women expressing regret after sharing intimacies with him. And certainly not after a kiss as explosive as the one they'd shared... But then he couldn't actually remember such an explosive moment with any woman.

Salim also had to admit—reluctantly—that he really didn't think it was a game, or a bluff designed to pique his interest. She'd meant it. In spite of the electric current that had sparked between them again as soon as he'd stepped into her room.

Her hair had still been deliciously tousled. Her lips swollen. Her shirt buttons had been done up wrong. He'd caught a glimpse of grey lace and just like that he'd become aroused all over again.

He'd resented the fact that she was the one inducing this crazy lust when he had a room full of beautiful uncomplicated women under his very roof, waiting for his attention.

But when he'd returned to the party, and been surrounded by sycophants and stunning women within minutes, he hadn't wanted any of them. And when he'd looked around and seen the elegant sheen on his guests wearing thin, he'd suddenly felt jaded and weary.

His conscience had tugged hard, and so he'd given instructions to his staff to start winding things down. He would have invited his cousin Riad to stay, but when he'd tried to call him he'd found a text message on his phone to say that Riad had already left with his mistress—something had come up at home that he had to attend to urgently.

There was movement in Salim's peripheral vision and he turned to see Charlotte approaching. His eyes widened as she came closer. She was wearing a long cream kaftan with gold edging that came to just below her knees, and beneath that she wore slim-fitting trousers in the same material. On her feet she wore low-heeled sandals.

He looked up and felt a spurt of something very disturbing when he saw that her hair was covered with a loose scarf, giving only a hint of that strawberry-blonde underneath.

He wanted to rip off the scarf, while at the same time feeling a possessive sense of satisfaction that her bright hair was hidden from other men. Impulses Salim had never ever experienced before.

There was something about her cool reserve and fresh-faced beauty that had sunk a hook inside him from the moment he'd seen her, and he knew it wouldn't let go until he'd had her.

Suddenly it was quite simple to Salim: he would bed her and she would lose her mystique, like every other woman he'd bedded.

She came to a stop a couple of feet away and put a hand to her head. 'What is it?'

Salim's voice was gruff when he said, 'You don't have to cover your head here.'

She pulled the scarf back and let it drop to her shoulders. Seeing the shining smooth cap of her hair made him remember what it had looked like after they'd kissed and his blood leapt. He had to restrain himself from perversely demanding that she cover it up again.

'Assa told me it's customary among most of the tribes for women to cover their heads.'

'Yes, and you can do it there.'

Salim's voice was curt and he saw how she flinched minutely. He cursed silently. He was on edge because of his unprecedented reaction to her, but also because he hadn't really acknowledged the possibility of meeting with the desert people of Tabat.

In the city it was easier to think of this as a business transaction—he was preparing this country to be strong so that it would flourish and thrive under new leadership. But now he would have to look into the eyes of those people, and it was as if he knew on some primal level that he was about to come face to face with himself in a way he'd never had to before.

And all under the cool green gaze of the woman looking at him now.

He opened the passenger door of the vehicle beside him. 'You'll travel with me.'

After a second when he thought she might argue Salim realised that, much as she provoked him, he found the prospect of her *not* being in close proximity to him was also unacceptable.

Eventually she moved towards the SUV and got in.

There was a flurry of activity as various bodyguards and staff finished packing away luggage and supplies in other vehicles.

Then Rafa approached Salim and bowed slightly, saying, 'Everything is ready, sire.'

Salim wanted to tell him not to bow, and not to call him sire, but he just nodded and got into the car himself, behind the steering wheel.

It was time to meet his destiny whether he liked it or not.

Charlotte could feel the tension rolling off Salim in waves and it surprised her. She'd assumed he would approach visiting the tribes with the same louche disregard with which he seemed to approach everything else. But he looked serious.

The city limits had been left far behind and there were at least three vehicles ahead of them and another three behind, carrying Rafa and Assa as well as other staff.

Nothing but endless sand stretched out all around them. Dunes rose and fell under the blinding sun and the horizon shimmered in the heat. Charlotte sent up silent thanks that they were protected by air-conditioning in the sturdy vehicle that navigated this shifting terrain easily.

Salim clearly didn't want to be making this trip. Charlotte took in his profile, which was effortlessly regal in spite of his reluctance to govern. He was wearing traditional robes, but hadn't made much more of an effort to clean up his appearance.

His hair was still wild and unruly, and Charlotte's fingers itched to see if it felt as silky and luxurious as it looked. She felt a crazy regret that she hadn't explored more when she'd had the chance. She clenched her hands into fists and ignored those itchy fingers.

But then her eye fell on his very stubbled jaw, and that made her think of how it had felt when he'd kissed her. The burn he'd left along her jaw…a physical brand. It made her wonder how it would feel on other parts of her body…

In a desperate bid to divert her mind, she asked, 'Why are you so reluctant to assume your role as king?'

His hand tightened on the wheel and the tension spiked. She thought he wasn't going to answer her when he was silent for so long, but then he said, 'I've already told you—I have numerous business concerns, thousands of employees. It's a role I never asked for or welcomed.'

'But…' Charlotte ignored the voice telling her to be quiet. 'No one asks to rule. They're born to rule.'

Salim's jaw tightened, but he kept his eyes on the road. 'That may be the case, but there's a better choice than me for Tabat.'

She assimilated what he'd just said and knew she should stay quiet but couldn't. She turned in her seat to face him. 'I don't think there is, actually. I think you know it's your destiny, and yet there's some other reason why you're so reluctant to take what's yours.'

Charlotte should have been alerted by the fact that the tension in the confined space suddenly changed and became more charged. Salim looked at her and let his eyes drift down over her body and immediately her blood sizzled.

'Believe me,' he drawled, 'I'm not reluctant to take what's mine at all.'

What's mine. He wasn't talking about Tabat. The thought that he considered her *his* was enough to render her speechless. No doubt exactly what he'd intended with this clever deflection.

Charlotte turned to face the front, locking her muscles tight against the betraying rush of arousal.

She refused to look at him for fear of what she'd see on his face. She'd learnt her lesson. She didn't care what this man's motivations were—she just wanted to get through the week unscathed.

Several hours later Salim was seated on a low chair in the tent of the local sheikh—the leader of the Rab'sah tribe. Charlotte had been right—the hospitality was so generous it was almost embarrassing. Even in spite of the cool reception Salim had received, which had been his due considering he hadn't come to visit them before now.

Their hospitality was even more overwhelming when he considered that they didn't have much. At all. There was a time when these nomadic tribes had had many riches—when they'd come into the city and bartered and sold precious gems and fat animals. But the world had marched on and left people like this behind, and it struck Salim somewhere very deeply now to see the aristocratic features and inherent pride of the tribe reduced to a mere shadow of its former self.

Charlotte wasn't in the tent, out of respect for the customs of the tribe that forbade women from attending formal meetings, and Salim welcomed the momentary space even as he hungered to lay his gaze on her.

He was still reeling from her far too perceptive observation earlier. No one had ever questioned his motives about anything before. No one had ever looked at him like that, as if trying to figure him out. Coming far too close to the bone.

So he told himself he was glad she wasn't here, and that ancient custom dictated women must be apart from the men, because he didn't care to be under her far too incisive green-eyed scrutiny as he listened to this sheikh and found himself feeling a sense of kinship that he'd never experienced before.

At dawn the following morning Charlotte was standing at the edge of the camp, watching as the sun rose in the east, slowly saturating the horizon with pink light. There was a low hum of activity behind her as the camp woke up, but there was an all-encompassing silence that surrounded her, deep and infinitely peaceful. Her instinct that she'd find the desert fascinating had been right.

'Bored yet?'

She started at the deep voice beside her and looked round to see Salim—tall and broad. He filled her vision in spite of the vast desert, and she realised that he truly fitted into this world even if he didn't want to. He was hewn from its very unforgiving landscape, from a long line of warriors.

She looked back out to the horizon, afraid he might see something of her fanciful thoughts on her face. 'I don't see how anyone could ever be bored here.'

'How did you sleep?'

In truth, she hadn't slept well. It might have been because she'd been sharing quarters with women and children, but they hadn't been the reason she'd lain awake. She'd been wondering about Salim, and about the fact that he was far more enigmatic than she'd ever anticipated.

She looked back at him and forced a bright smile. 'Like a log—and you?'

He smiled too, showing his teeth. 'Like a log.'

The hell he had. He'd spent hours alternating between ignoring his guilty conscience and battling images of this woman with her shirt undone and one pale plump breast filling his palm. That soft lush mouth under his.

The rising sun was bathing her in a warm glow. She was dressed traditionally again. Her hair peeped out from under the veil she wore. Her face was bare of make-up. He could see freckles. He couldn't remember the last time he'd seen such fresh-faced beauty.

The way she got to him made him ask caustically, 'You're not missing your home comforts too much?'

It rankled with him now that he knew she'd had to share a tent with some of the higher born women and children and yet it didn't seem to have fazed her in the slightest.

Those green eyes sparked and Salim felt an answering fire burn deep in his core. More than lust. Disturbing.

She folded her arms and faced him. 'Still trying to get rid of me?'

No way.

The strength of that assertion surprised him. He clamped his mouth shut in case it slipped out.

When he didn't respond, she said, 'Look, I told you—I've travelled. It's a privilege to spend time with people like these.' She sounded exasperated.

He'd seen her yesterday, sitting cross-legged with a group of women, smiling and conversing with them as best she could, given the differences in dialect. She'd looked utterly comfortable and graceful in spite of her dusty clothes and very basic surroundings. And they'd looked at her with awe.

She turned now and Salim's chest tightened. She'd looked so serene and peaceful standing there, watching the sunrise. He'd intruded because he'd been envious of that peace and absorption. And because he'd wanted her attention on *him*.

He put a hand on her arm and she stopped, looking at him warily. He cursed himself for not just letting her go.

'Did you want something?'

He let her arm go. 'Just to say we'll be leaving shortly.'

She nodded after a moment. 'I'll be ready.'

Salim turned back to face the desert and had an uncomfortable skin-prickling sense of foreboding that this trip was not going to pan out as he'd planned it.

At all.

By day three Charlotte was surprised at how easily she'd settled into the rhythm of moving from place to place. And at how little she missed civilisation. As they had moved deeper and deeper into the desert she'd found herself unwinding, helpless not to do so in the face of a much more primeval rhythm.

The evening was closing in over the oasis that was the current base for the Jadar tribe—one of the oldest in the region. It was where the name Jandor had come from, when this tribe's ancestors had sacked and invaded the city.

She walked through the camp back to her tent after meeting with the tribe's leaders. This tribe was different from most and run on more egalitarian lines. Women were just as much a part of important discussions as men and they didn't wear veils, so Charlotte had left hers off and relished the breeze through her hair now.

During the meetings Charlotte had been surprised at how deferential Salim had been, and how attentive. She'd expected to find herself cringing as he made his reluctance to be there known, but he'd been effortlessly respectful while also displaying an innate sense of authority that had nothing to do with arrogance.

She'd just returned to her small tent, and was unpacking her bag, appreciating the thought of her own private space for the first time in three nights, when a noise made her look round.

Assa was at the opening of the tent and she said, 'King Al-Noury would like you to join him for dinner in his tent.'

Even though he wasn't yet crowned, his people already called him king.

Charlotte's belly flipped. She'd managed to more or less avoid him since the other morning, keeping their conversation to a minimum as they travelled from place to place. But her awareness of him was increasing exponentially. Along with her confusion that he wasn't behaving as she might have expected.

What could Charlotte say? She'd been summoned by the king. 'Of course. I'll just change quickly.'

The fine desert sand seemed to get everywhere, so Charlotte availed herself of the small bathroom attached to the tent and refreshed herself and changed into a clean set of trousers and a tunic. When she re-emerged Assa was waiting to show her to Salim's tent.

Darkness had fallen over the camp and there were familiar sounds of rattling plates and utensils, fractious children crying and soothing voices.

Charlotte absorbed the nomadic atmosphere of the camp. Mouth-watering smells of cooking reminded her she hadn't eaten in a few hours. She stopped and smiled when some small children ran around her as they played a game of catch before disappearing behind one of the tents.

Strangely, because she'd never thought of herself as being remotely maternal—especially after her experiences at the hands of her self-absorbed mother and absent father—she was taken completely unawares by a pang of yearning, and when she saw Assa waiting for her outside a much larger tent, with golden light spilling out into the camp, she realised far too belatedly that she was not ready to face Salim's all too blistering blue gaze.

But, as if hearing her thoughts, Salim appeared in the entrance of the tent, easily filling the space. 'Please, come in.'

And she had to keep moving forward, pushing that alien emotion down.

When she walked into his tent her jaw dropped and she forgot everything for a moment. It was like something out of an Arabian fantasy. Luxurious floor-coverings, sumptuous soft furnishings in bright jewel colours. A dining area that wouldn't have looked out of place in a Parisian restaurant and a bed that Charlotte couldn't take her eyes off. It dominated the space and was covered in silk and satin, with muslin drapes around it, fluttering in the light breeze.

She'd never have guessed from the rest of the far more humble camp that this could exist.

'It's a bit much, isn't it?'

Charlotte managed to tear her gaze from the bed to look at Salim, who was wincing slightly. Feeling something light bubble up inside her she asked innocently, 'Not to your specifications, then?'

He looked at her and his mouth tipped up wryly. 'No.'

He gestured for her to take a seat at the dining table, and she said as she watched him take a seat opposite her, 'Let me guess—you're into stark minimalism and masculine colours? Abstract art?'

He flicked out a linen napkin. 'You say that like it's a bad thing.'

A moment shimmered between them, light and fragile, and then he said, 'You looked as if you'd just seen a ghost when you walked in—I hope that wasn't a reaction to my invitation.'

Charlotte avoided his eye for a moment, placing her own napkin on her lap. When she looked up again he was watching her with a narrowed gaze. She heard noises coming from the back of the tent, the sounds and smells of dinner. It helped to lessen the feeling of being in a lavish cocoon with this man.

She shrugged minutely. 'I just noticed something... walking through the camp. A real sense of community that you don't find in many places any more.'

Salim said, 'You do seem at home here. And I'm sure you don't need me to tell you this, but you're a natural diplomat. I've watched how you put everyone at ease and can converse equally with a sheikh or the girl washing the dishes.'

Ridiculously, Charlotte blushed at Salim's praise— even though she knew without false modesty that she was good at her job. 'Thank you. This part of the world has always been fascinating to me.'

They were interrupted by staff appearing with a tray of delicious-smelling food. When they were alone again Salim held up a bottle of red wine and said, 'May I?'

Charlotte felt as if she needed the sustenance so she nodded. He filled her glass and she took a sip.

There was a big bowl of food to be shared—Salim

explained that it was chicken mixed with couscous, spices, herbs and bread.

Charlotte filled her plate.

They ate in silence for a few minutes, both savouring the food, but then Salim sat back and said, 'So that sense of community...did you grow up in a small town?'

Charlotte's insides tensed automatically. She cursed her inability to lie and hoped he'd lose interest when she said, as perfunctorily as she could, 'No, I grew up in London. I was an only child and my parents divorced when I was young. I spent a lot of time in boarding schools and with nannies.'

'So you knew the opposite of community, then?' he observed, with a perspicacity that was as unwelcome as it was insightful.

Charlotte put down her fork and took another sip of wine, relishing the slight headiness it brought, which made her feel reckless enough to respond mockingly, 'I was a poor little rich girl. My parents were millionaires, which afforded them the luxury of having their child taken care of. But their lifestyles have never appealed to me. I wanted to make my own way. I don't depend on them for anything.'

She couldn't help the pride showing in her voice when she said that.

His gaze narrowed on her and she fought against squirming in her chair. Why did he have to look at her like that? As if he could see right through her?

'We have something in common. I never relished the cushion of my family's fortune. I also wanted to make my own way. I worked my way through college and everything I own now is mine and mine alone.'

She asked, 'Is that why you're reluctant to let it all go and become king?'

Salim was shocked he'd said so much, and that he'd felt the need to let her know that he appreciated her independence because he shared it. The sense of kinship was unsettling.

He shrugged, hiding how accurately her words had hit him. 'Perhaps it's part of it. Along with the responsibility I feel.'

He stopped there, before he let the real reasons slip out. He hadn't prepared for this as his brother had so assiduously. He'd allowed a rift to grow between them, so how could he unite a country? And how could he protect the people of Tabat when he hadn't been able to save his own sister?

Before she could ask any more far too pertinent questions, Salim asked, 'What about you? What drove you to become a diplomat and turn your back on the life of being an heiress?'

She avoided his eye for so long that he thought she wasn't going to answer, but then she looked at him and it was like a punch to his gut. There was something so...unguarded about her expression.

'It was my parents,' she said quietly. 'Their divorce was ugly. They used me as a pawn to score points off each other, but once my mother had custody she pretty much abandoned me. I realised at a young age that unconditional love and family happiness are an illusion. So I decided to distance myself as much as possible— become independent so they could never use me as a pawn again.'

Salim was a little speechless. He'd thought his parents were cold automatons, but evidently they hadn't been the only ones. 'Does your aversion to Christmas have anything to do with all that?'

Her eyes widened and her mouth opened before she'd recovered. 'How did you know?'

He shrugged, not liking how easily he'd intuited that. 'A guess. It's a time of year that evokes strong re-actions, and you were pretty adamant that you didn't mind missing it.'

She glanced down at her napkin, folding it over and over. Salim wanted to put his hand over hers, but curled it into a fist to stop himself.

She stopped fidgeting and looked at him. 'They di-vorced just before Christmas. Days before.'

Some of the candles had gone out, making the light in the tent dimmer. The delicate lines of her face when she looked at him were in sharp relief. Her eyes were huge.

'Go on,' he said, aware of the irony. He never usu-ally encouraged women to reveal anything more than the most superficial parts of their lives to him. But this woman intrigued him.

'Since then I've invariably spent Christmas on my own. Whenever the head of my boarding school knew I was due to spend the holiday alone, because my mother was working or abroad, they'd ask a family to take me in... I went once or twice, but no matter how welcome they made me feel it only made me more conscious of not being a part of a family.'

'What about your father?'

She shrugged. 'I only saw him a handful of times after I chose my mother to be my prime carer in the divorce.'

She smiled then, but it was tight, almost derisory.

'The really sad thing, though, is that as much as I hate Christmas, I love it too. The Christmas before the divorce was perfect. Just the three of us in a cottage in

Devon. It snowed that year, and my father dressed up as Santa Claus, and my mother showed him to me, tip-toeing away from the house as if he'd just left his gifts. It was magical...'

Charlotte's gaze focused on Salim again and she felt the blood drain from her face as she realised just how much she'd revealed. His expression was inscrutable in the flickering golden light of the candles. As if he cared about her sad tale! What was wrong with her? She never spoke of her past—not if she could help it—and certainly not with someone who made her feel so many conflicting emotions and desires.

She stood up abruptly, dropping her napkin. 'I should go to bed—it's been a long day. Thank you for dinner.'

She wanted to get out of that decadent and confined space *now*. And away from those blue eyes. She was burning up from the inside out and it wasn't just from embarrassment. It was from sitting in such close prox-imity to Salim's lazily coiled sexual magnetism.

Salim stood up too, putting down his own napkin. He was watching her warily, which made her feel even more exposed as she stepped away from the table.

She'd turned and was almost at the entrance to the tent when her hand was caught in a much bigger one and her heart leapt into her throat. She hadn't even heard him move, the sound muffled by the sumptuous carpets. She turned around and tried to pull her hand free, but he held it too firmly.

She could feel her pulse fluttering against his fin-ger. 'What is it?'

Why did she sound so breathless?

Salim looked very tall and dark in the dim golden light. More like a warrior than ever.

'Don't go back to your tent, Charlotte, stay here to-night.'

Charlotte didn't even register what Salim had said for a minute. Without thinking, she responded automatically, 'But why? That's where I'm…'

And then she stuttered to a stop as comprehension started to sink in and the heat in his eyes made his meaning very explicit. Everything about his suggestion screamed *danger* to Charlotte, even as she could feel the betraying evidence of the effect he'd had on her all evening.

His finger moved back and forth on her wrist, over her pulse point. Hypnotising her. All her muscles pulled taut, and at the same time seemed to soften.

And then she thought of spilling her guts with little or no encouragement. She remembered the burn of embarrassment and it burned even more now at the thought that he might have manipulated her into opening up so he could take advantage of her emotional vulnerability.

A little voice mocked her that he wouldn't have to resort to such crude tactics, but she ignored it.

She pulled her hand free. 'You think that I'll just fall into your bed because you ask?'

A muscle ticked in his jaw. 'You know what there is between us—it's off the charts.'

The kiss.

She stiffened. 'We agreed that was a mistake…inappropriate. That it wouldn't happen again.'

He shook his head. 'No, *you* said it wouldn't happen again. But you're lying to yourself if you think you can resist this… We have amazing chemistry. We're both adults. We're never going to see each other again once the coronation is over. There's no reason why this can't happen.'

Yes, there is! A hysterical voice resounded inside Charlotte. And it was because of what he'd just said: *'We're never going to see each other again'.*

Of course they wouldn't. A woman like Charlotte would never feature in this man's life and that shouldn't matter to her. But already it did. And it shouldn't. It couldn't.

A million and one emotions landed in Charlotte's belly, the strongest of which was an intense feeling of vulnerability. He had no idea how innocent she was. Evidently he thought that telling her he wanted her was enough to have her swooning at his feet in gratitude...

Feeling very defensive, but not wanting him to see how he'd got to her, she said as coolly as she could, 'I'm afraid I don't agree with your assessment of the situation. Goodnight, Salim.'

She cringed inwardly. She sounded like an accountant.

Salim looked at her for a long moment, his expression unreadable. And then he just said, 'Very well. Goodnight, Charlotte.'

He reached past her to pull back the heavy drapes covering the entrance and the cool night-time desert breeze skated over her skin. She hated the treacherous part of her that wasn't exactly heartened to see this gentlemanly side of him. Where was the stereotypical playboy who wouldn't take no for an answer because she'd bruised his pride?

She quickly turned and fled, before she could give herself away. Before he could see how conflicted she was. No other person had ever pushed her buttons so effectively, and when she got back to her own tent she paced up and down, sensations and emotions boiling over too much to relax.

She should be feeling triumphant—she'd just turned down one of the sexiest and most arrogant men in the world. She'd stood up to him. But she hated to admit now that it felt like a hollow victory.

Eventually she did sit down on the bed and noticed vaguely that someone—Assa?—had come in and lit some lamps and turned the bed down. A far less lavish version of Salim's...where, if she'd said yes, they might be entwined right now...

She stood up again and busied herself undressing and getting ready for bed, ignoring the ache that spread through her whole body from her core.

She busied herself to avoid thinking about the real reason she'd turned Salim down: because she was still a virgin.

It was something she was subconsciously aware of but had managed to successfully ignore for a long time. She'd been so focused on her career—

She stopped, catching her reflection in the mirror over the sink where she was about to wash herself.

Her cheeks were flushed bright red and her neat shoulder-length bob was a lot less sleek than usual. She was pathetic. The reason she was a virgin had nothing to do with her career and everything to do with the fact that she was too afraid to let anyone close enough to hurt her as much as her parents had.

But when she thought about Salim's arrogant proposal just now—yes, arrogant—the last thing she'd been afraid of was getting hurt. It had been the fear of incineration if he kissed her again. The fear of exposure. And the fear of his look of incredulity if he found out how innocent she was. She doubted a man like that had ever slept with a virgin in his life.

He'd summed her up from the start as uptight. He would laugh in her face if he knew how right he was.

She'd already told Salim far too much this evening. She wasn't going to bare herself—literally—even more. He wasn't worth risking her precious independence for. *He wasn't*, she told herself fiercely as she did her best to ignore the ache, which only seemed to grow more acute.

CHAPTER FIVE

'It LOOKS LIKE we'll have to stay here for a couple of days.'

'Oh, no—why?' Charlotte looked at Assa and felt panicky.

They'd been due to return to Tabat City the following morning, and frankly she couldn't wait to get back. The vast desert now felt as oppressive as a small confined space after enduring Salim's civil yet cool demeanour since they'd arrived at their last stop, the oasis camp of the Wahir tribe, earlier that day.

That morning, when Rafa had asked if Salim minded if he joined him in the car to discuss matters of state on the journey from Jadar, Charlotte had jumped at the opportunity to escape and had taken Rafa's place in his own transport.

The intense look Salim had sent her still made her shiver. She didn't want to know what he might have said to her if they'd been alone. She'd vowed not to be alone with him ever again.

Since they'd arrived, Salim had been in intense discussion with the Wahir tribe's leaders. Charlotte had been allowed to sit in on the meetings, concentrating hard to follow the very stylised Arabic they used. Once again she'd been surprised to note that Salim was respectful and attentive.

Assa said, 'I don't mind staying another night if we have to—it's as beautiful here as everyone said it was.'

Charlotte was pulled out of her spiralling thoughts. Assa was right: this camp was the most picturesque they'd been to yet. A beautiful green oasis with palm trees and a huge pool of clear green water.

'Why do we have to stay?'

The young girl looked at her, her dark eyes huge. 'They say a sandstorm will hit tonight, and if it does it'll take at least another day to unearth all the vehicles to travel back to Tabat.'

'Can't they avoid that happening?' Charlotte asked weakly, knowing she was being ridiculous. A meteorological event was hardly negotiable.

'We're on high ground, Miss McQuillan, but there's no escaping the power of a storm.'

Assa took an armful of Charlotte's dirty laundry—in spite of her protests that she could wash her own things—and turned at the opening of the tent.

'You'll come to the wedding later, won't you? It would be considered very rude not to as an honoured guest.'

'Of course,' Charlotte answered.

All the king's entourage had been invited to attend the wedding of the oldest daughter of the tribe's leader and Charlotte was intrigued, having never witnessed a Bedouin wedding before. There was an air of great excitement in the camp, and Charlotte had noticed that there were a lot more people there than there had been earlier.

Charlotte had every intention of making sure she stayed well out of Salim's way, and if a sandstorm hit overnight she'd be one of the first helping to unearth the vehicles in the morning.

* * *

Salim was acutely conscious of the ritual he was witnessing in a way that he might not have anticipated before embarking on this trip. Taking place in front of him was a centuries-old custom designed to bind families and neighbouring tribes together in a way that would unify them and promote peace in a place where wars had once been rife and deadly.

He was surprised at the strength of an echo inside him that recognised and accepted this on some deep level, in spite of doing his damnedest to deny that he was part of this history and culture.

Destiny. The hated word slid into his mind, but for once it didn't induce the same level of rejection as it normally did. The truth was that he came from these people. His ancestors had said these same words, more or less.

For the first time Salim felt a sense of belonging he'd never experienced before creep over him. As if ancient and invisible bindings were slowly but inexorably wrapping around him like tentacles and tying him to the life he was so determined to reject. As if *he* was a nomad who was returning home.

It was an unsettling thought, but not even that was unsettling enough to distract him from the woman who sat at his right-hand side, who had turned him down him so summarily the previous evening.

His body had started humming as soon as she'd sat down beside him, enveloping him with a delicate and tantalising scent that made him think of cool green moss and much earthier things, like tangling naked on a soft surface.

Thankfully his voluminous robe hid the near-constant state of arousal he had little control over, which irritated him greatly. Salim usually had no problem mastering his physical impulses, no matter how attractive the woman. But of course no other woman had proved so elusive.

Charlotte had studiously avoided his eye since she'd arrived, just as she'd been studiously avoiding him all day. He'd observed her earlier, talking earnestly with both the women and the men of the tribe in Arabic. The ease she felt with them and their acceptance of her made him all at once proud and yet perversely annoyed that his diplomatic expert was being so...diplomatic.

The couple in front of them were seated face to face on cushions, about to say their vows. Salim gave in to an urge too great for him to resist and looked at Charlotte. He noticed with another spurt of irritation that she was quite oblivious to him.

After the confidences she'd shared last night—that *they'd* shared—he should be the one pushing her away. And yet at every moment when she'd avoided his eye today, or evaded him, it had only fired up a primal urge to hunt her down.

Her green eyes were suspiciously shiny now, and he followed her gaze back to the young couple to see that the woman's hands were together in the prayer position and the man was placing the wedding ring over each of her fingers until he got to the ring finger.

The young man looked at the woman and said in Arabic as he slid the ring down her finger, 'I marry you, I marry you, I marry you,' as was this particular tribe's custom in marriage. Then she repeated his words and actions.

Now they were married. It was that simple.

They could be separated as easily, by saying the words *I divorce you* three times in front of the tribe leader, but from the way the young man was looking at his bride, and she back at him, this was a love match.

Salim's characteristic cynicism was curiously elusive.

Everyone stood up and started to cheer, and the happy young couple were shepherded out to their nuptial tent with great catcalling and fanfare.

Salim stood and put a hand out to help Charlotte stand. She looked up and he saw a definite glistening in those huge eyes before she dipped her head and smoothly rose, ignoring his hand.

His irritation at her dogged rejection was made sharper by the way the scene he'd just witnessed had sneaked under his well-worn guard.

Charlotte was turning to go and, incensed that she might evade him so easily, Salim caught her hand so she had to stop and look at him.

The lingering brightness in her eyes impacted on him in a way he didn't welcome. To cover it up, he drawled mockingly, 'Why, I do believe you're a romantic.'

'You're a romantic.'

Charlotte stiffened under his hand. A panicky feeling made her chest tight. The last thing she was was a romantic. She'd *told* Salim that she'd learnt her lessons young. That she had no illusions. And yet he didn't believe her because he could see how witnessing that achingly simple and yet profound ceremony just now—seeing the pretty girl with her elaborate wedding headdress and the dark kohl around her eyes—had affected Charlotte before she'd even absorbed the fullness of that revelation herself.

Avoiding him all day felt like an utterly futile exercise now. He was in her mind and under her skin.

Just then Rafa appeared at Salim's other side and,

taking advantage of his momentary distraction, Charlotte pulled her hand free and fled out of the tent behind the crowd without saying a word.

She was barely aware of the fact that the wind had started whipping up since the ceremony had started, or that there was a sense of urgency as people ran from tent to tent, shouting things to each other. She made her way instinctively to the natural pool and stood at the edge, breathing hard and trying to control her rising panic.

She wasn't a romantic. *She wasn't*.

So why had that ceremony affected her so profoundly? She knew the answer—fatally. It was rooted in that place where she still yearned for an idyllic Christmas and a happy family...

The choppy water mirrored her choppy emotions. She was still captivated, in spite of herself, by the thought that you could just look at someone and say those three words three times and it was done.

Charlotte hated it that Salim had been a witness to her moment of vulnerable revelation. Thinking of the way he'd drawled *'You're a romantic'* scored at her insides again.

She went cold all over as something else struck her—something far more threatening and disturbing. The thought of Salim telling himself that the reason she'd refused to sleep with him was because she wanted *more*.

Anger rose, whipping up inside her the way the wind was now whipping at her hair and her clothes. She turned around, galvanised by the thought of wiping that mocking look off Salim's face, and made her way back through the camp, which was now eerily empty.

Salim's tent stood tall and imposing, apart from the

camp, and she made straight for it, grabbing the heavy material covering the doorway and pulling it back to step into the space.

Immediately she was aware of the wind being muffled and a sense of stillness. Once again the tent was decadently furnished—like something from a lavish movie set. Candles threw out a golden glow, imbuing the space with warmth and luxury.

As the silence settled around her she realised she'd made a huge mistake, but before she could turn and escape she heard a sound and Salim stepped out from behind a screen on the other side of the tent.

Charlotte couldn't move.

He was naked.

Or almost naked. A tiny towel was hitched around his slim waist and his skin gleamed like burnished bronze. His hair was wet. He'd obviously just had a shower.

All Charlotte could see was the massive expanse of broad muscled chest and more ridges of muscle that led down to the towel, which did precious little to hide the very healthy bulge underneath, and then down lower to powerful thighs and strong legs.

If she'd thought he looked like a warrior before, now she realised he was a god. She was rooted to the spot, as if she'd never seen a naked man in the flesh before. Because she hadn't.

That realisation made her whirl around to leave, but in her agitation she couldn't find the opening of the tent. She was almost crying with frustration when she felt a solid presence behind her, and then a hand wrapped itself over her arm and turned her around.

She closed her eyes. Her heart was thumping so hard she felt light-headed.

'Open your eyes, Charlotte.'

With the utmost reluctance she did, and then felt a mixture of relief and regret to see that he'd thrown on a tunic. She couldn't lift her eyes higher, though, not wanting to see the expression on his face. But of course he tipped up her chin and she had no choice.

His face was harder than she'd ever seen it, those blue eyes burning. As if *he* was angry. When she was the angry one. She'd just forgotten for a moment.

She stepped back, dislodging his hold on her. She felt crowded and moved around him to gain some space.

He turned, watching her. 'Was there something you wished to discuss, Charlotte?'

She folded her arms, lifted her chin and hoped her voice wouldn't betray her. 'There was, actually. For your information, I am most certainly not a romantic. Nothing could be further from the truth.'

Salim folded his arms too, mirroring her defensive stance. 'So what was that back there? Some dust in your eye?'

He didn't believe her. She had to make him understand. 'I was six when my parents divorced. It was ugly and very public.'

He frowned. 'What do you mean? How public?'

Charlotte gave a short harsh laugh. 'As public as you can get. My father is Harry Lassiter and my mother is Louise Lassiter—she didn't change her name after the divorce.'

Salim's gaze sharpened. 'The award-winning movie director and the actress?'

Charlotte nodded. They'd both won multiple awards for the film, which had brought them together in the first place.

Salim's frown deepened. 'But you're Charlotte Mc-Quillan.'

Her arms tightened around herself. Already she was regretting opening her mouth. What was it about this man that made him her confessor?

'I changed my name legally as soon as I turned eighteen. I took my grandmother's maiden name. I didn't want to be associated with my parents, or the most infamous divorce in the last couple of decades.'

Salim said, 'I was too young for it to be on my radar at the time, but I remember reading about it later.'

Charlotte grew hot, thinking of the lurid exposé programme that had been made about it, which was still on endless repeat on the entertainment channels. The memory of the pack of press waiting outside the courtroom was still vivid, and the awful knowledge that she'd wet herself because she'd been so upset after her father had said to her in the courtroom, *'You're no longer my daughter,'* because she'd chosen to stay with her mother.

Her tights had been stuck to her legs, damp and clammy, and she'd been sure that everyone would know her shame.

Diverting her mind from too-painful memories, she said, 'I'm just telling you this so that you'll understand why I have no illusions about romance or love.'

A sharp pain lanced her as she recalled the wedding ceremony she'd just witnessed and the well of secret emotion it had tapped into. She felt as if she'd just betrayed something precious.

Salim said, 'I couldn't agree more. My experiences might not have been the same as yours, but the end result is the same.'

Charlotte blinked at him. Bizarrely, his words didn't make her feel comforted.

He said tautly, 'My parents hated each other. You say you were a pawn—well, so were my brother and I. Born to lead two countries and keep the peace.'

Charlotte's insides twisted as she imagined growing up in that environment. 'People have been born for a lot less.'

He smiled, but it was hard. 'Yes, but they have their freedom.' And then his smile faded. 'Maybe we're not so different after all, hmm?'

Charlotte looked at Salim incredulously, thinking that they couldn't be *more* different. He was vital and arrogant, a force to be reckoned with, and she... Who was she? Someone who'd spent her life running from feeling rejected and abandoned, building a persona to protect herself from all that.

It suddenly felt very fragile. She felt exposed and raw, from those memories and from saying too much. Again.

She backed away. 'I'm sorry. I shouldn't have come here.'

'Wait. Stop.'

There was a note of command in his voice that stopped her in her tracks.

'Why did you come here this evening, really?'

Charlotte swallowed. Her skin felt tight and hot and her mouth was dry. Her heart was beating like a trapped bird against her chest.

'Just as I told you—I wanted to make sure you knew that I don't...don't have romantic notions.'

Salim moved towards her and she was rooted to the ground. 'Why is that so important?'

She swallowed again. 'I didn't want you to think

that I refused you last night because I wanted something more. I don't want more…' She stopped, her heart beating too hard and her brain fusing and stopping her words.

Because she was afraid she was lying to herself.

The wind screeched outside. Salim's eyes were like two blue flames. 'Believe me, the last thing you inspire is feelings of romance…'

Charlotte felt a pang of hurt. 'I don't?'

He shook his head. 'No. You inspire much earthier things. Dark and decadent things.'

There was still a couple of feet between them, but Charlotte felt as if Salim was touching her. The push and pull inside her was torture.

For a second she almost took a step towards him, giving in to the inexorable pull. But sanity prevailed. She was a virgin. She was no match for this man's presumably expert and voracious appetites. He would laugh at her, would ridicule her.

Before she could lose her mind completely, Charlotte blurted out, 'I'm going back to my tent.'

She turned abruptly and blindly felt for the opening of the tent, but nothing happened when she tried to open it. Panic mounted, and then she heard Salim's voice.

'We're in the middle of a sandstorm. The tent has been secured for our safety. If you were to step outside right now you'd be flayed in minutes.'

Charlotte noticed far too belatedly that the entire structure of the tent was swaying alarmingly. She dropped her hands and turned around.

Salim had a suspiciously innocent look on his face. 'Don't worry, we're quite safe. These tents are built to withstand such events.'

Charlotte almost couldn't articulate words, but she forced them out. 'So, what does that mean.?'

An unmistakable glint of something wicked in Salim's eyes replaced any hint of innocence on his handsome face. 'It means, Charlotte, that you'll have to spend the night here.'

CHAPTER SIX

CHARLOTTE TOOK A deep breath as she looked at herself in the small ornate mirror that hung—swinging precariously now—over the sink in the sectioned off bathing area of the tent. She looked wild. Her hair had been blown everywhere by the wind.

She tried to drum up a sense of horror seeing herself come so undone, but in truth when Salim had told her she'd have to stay there a very illicit sense of liberation had flowed into her blood, making it race. As if nature itself had colluded to take the angst she was feeling out of her belly and replace it with a sense of fatalism.

She couldn't keep fighting this. No matter how terrifying it was.

Salim hadn't been crass enough actually to articulate what might happen, but it throbbed in the air even now.

Just then, as if to test her, something soft and light-coloured was flicked over the screen separating her from the rest of the tent and Salim's voice floated in, far too close for comfort.

'You can use this after you wash. It'll be too big but it's all I have.'

Charlotte was about to open to her mouth to declare she didn't need to change, because she had no intention of taking off a stitch of her clothing, no matter what was going on in her head and body, but the words stuck in her throat when she found herself wondering if *he* had worn this tunic.

Weakly, she said nothing and pulled it over the screen into her hands. His scent drifted tantalisingly from the folds of material and something tugged deep in her belly—an ache that had become all too familiar since she'd met Salim.

She looked at herself in the mirror—her expression was one of someone who was hunted. Or *haunted*, to be more accurate. Haunted by her past.

It struck her then—as much as she'd done her best to move away from it—her past was still nipping at her heels, dictating everything she did. Stopping her from living fully for fear of annihilation. Rejection.

She thought she'd distanced herself from any possibility of pain, but she realised now with a sense of futility that you could never really escape pain. Unless you wanted to live half a life. And she knew now that she wanted more than that—even if it meant taking a risk.

The wind howled outside and the sense of being closed off from everything was very seductive. It whispered at her to let go of her inhibitions. It whispered at her to take a risk.

'Charlotte? Is everything all right?'

She jumped at Salim's voice and then answered quickly, 'Everything is fine. I'll be out in a minute.'

A reckless excitement filled her in that moment—a sense of seizing something vital and alive. Without really thinking about the invisible line she'd stepped over in her own mind, Charlotte stripped and stepped into the shower area, leaving her own clothes in a neat pile on a chair.

Hot water rained down over her head and body and

she tipped her face up. She couldn't help but be aware of the symbolism; she felt as if a layer of her carefully constructed persona was being washed away too.

She was in the middle of the desert in the middle of a sandstorm, sharing a tent with a man who had got under her skin and made her want more than she'd ever wanted in her life.

When she stepped out and dried herself perfunctorily with a towel cool air made her skin pop up into goose-bumps. Her nipples were hard and tight. The ache deep in her core intensified.

The tunic Salim had given her fell heavily down her naked body, pooling on the ground at her feet. It had a vee neck that on him would look perfectly civilised, but on her cut right between her breasts, showing an indecent amount of flesh.

Suddenly Charlotte didn't care. It was as if she could see her habitual self stalking out of this space, still dressed in her own clothes, determined to resist at all costs, but she didn't want to be her any more. Or at least not for tonight.

The earth was being whipped into a frenzy outside, and they were separated from that awesome power by only a flimsy barrier. It intensified her growing urgency to seize the moment.

Charlotte took a breath and stepped out from behind the screen. For a second she couldn't see anything in the dimly lit space, and her very recent and nebulous bravado faltered. But then her eyes fell on the bed, and she saw the unmistakably masculine shape of Salim, sprawled in careless abandon on top of the sumptuous fabrics.

The tent around them groaned ominously, but he didn't move. Hardly breathing, Charlotte picked up the excess folds of the robe in one hand and moved forward, coming to a stop a few feet from the bed.

When her eyes had finally adjusted to the light she saw that he wasn't moving because he was asleep, his dark lashes resting on those slashing high aristocratic cheekbones. Even though he wore clothes—he'd thrown trousers on under his robe—the latent power of that impressive body was impossible to conceal.

There was something incredibly voyeuristic about watching him in this moment of rare defencelessness, but that wasn't strictly accurate because even now he exuded an air of force and control.

His leg moved slightly and Charlotte panicked, reality slamming into her like cold bucket of water. What was she doing? Had she really expected to walk out here and find him waiting for her just because he'd said, *'You'll have to spend the night here'* with that glint in his eye? Expected that he would still want her?

He was just toying with her because she was a woman unlike his other lovers—someone who intrigued him briefly. She was an idiot to think that anything fundamental had changed within her so that she was ready to throw caution to the winds, and she sent up silent thanks now that he'd never know how close she'd come to making a complete fool of herself.

She turned around to escape behind the screen, but got no further than a couple of feet when she heard Salim say, 'Where are you going?'

Salim pushed himself up to sit on the bed. Charlotte had her back to him. He'd been listening to the sounds of the shower and imagining rivulets of water running down over her slender pale body. Then he'd heard her steal softly into the tent and he'd feigned sleep, curious to see what she'd do...

But nothing had happened and when he'd opened his eyes she'd been walking away.

She slowly turned around to face him.

Salim stood up from the bed. The robe he'd given her was comically large on her slender frame, but comical was the last thing he was feeling as he took her in.

She was bathed in the golden light of the candles around her and it made her pale skin even more lustrous. Her hair was damp and curling from the shower. And when his gaze dipped down desire engulfed him in a hot wave.

He'd seen women dressed in the most provocative lingerie the world had to offer. And yet right now the woman in front of him was the most erotic vision he'd ever seen.

The vee of the robe came to just below Charlotte's breasts and did little to conceal the high, firm swells. He could see the outline of her body through the light material—where her waist dipped in and her hips flared out, her long legs and the slightly darker juncture between them.

His mouth watered at the prospect of tasting her there, feeling her come apart in his mouth…

She looked like the kind of woman he'd never slept with in his life. Like an innocent. And, as much as he knew he should turn away from her because he had no right corrupting anyone's innocence, the dark part of him wanted her too much. The dark part of him he'd spent a lifetime indulging to carve out his independence, further his ambitions and seek revenge.

Charlotte couldn't turn back now—not under Salim's hungry gaze. It emboldened her again. She felt as if he'd just touched her all over but it wasn't enough. She wanted him to touch her…properly.

She moved across the tent to stand in front of him, light-headed with what she was doing. She said, before she could stop herself, 'What you said…that I make you want earthy things, dark things… I want that too.'

Salim's gaze locked onto her mouth and she could see the colour slash across his cheeks. He lifted a hand and rubbed his thumb across her lower lip, his fingers touching her jaw. She held her breath, acutely aware of her innocence. Should she say something?

Her gut clenched.

Surely, she told herself, a man like him would hardly be sensitive enough to perceive her innocence. And there was some bizarre comfort in the fact that her first lover would be a man who wouldn't feel the need to give her platitudes or false promises.

She didn't want someone tender and caring, as she'd always believed. She craved this inferno of need and she wanted it with this man who stood head and shoulders above every other man she'd ever met.

She was under no illusions. She knew that this was a moment out of time, that they were cocooned in this tent while a storm raged outside. In their usual world and in their usual circumstances he wouldn't have looked at her twice, and she felt greedy now. Greedy to store up this moment for when they would be back in the real world.

He took his thumb off her mouth and put his hands on her arms. Blue eyes on green. 'Are you sure?'

She nodded. A faint alarm bell was ringing at his consideration, but it was too faint to be heard right now.

He brought his hands up her arms to her shoulders and slipped his fingers under the material of the robe. With gentle pressure he pushed at the robe until it slipped down her shoulders, baring them. It clung precariously to her upper arms and the slopes of her breasts for an infinitesimal moment, but when Salim exerted more pressure it fell all the way to the ground and pooled at her feet.

She was naked in front of him, more exposed than she'd ever been, but fire was burning inside her, and a hitherto unexplored sense of feminine power.

Salim's gaze dropped down over her body, slowly and thoroughly. His eyes lingered on her breasts, which she'd always felt were too small. Now they felt positively voluptuous under his inspection. And then his gaze dropped further, and the ache between her legs turned sharp and insistent.

She didn't realise she was trembling until he stepped back and started to take off his tunic, pulling it over his head and revealing that impressive chest again. With deft movements he shed his trousers and now he was naked too. Charlotte couldn't help herself. Her eyes widened as she took in the majestic virility of the man in front of her.

She felt as if something was slotting into place—as if she'd had the desire to see this visual since the moment she'd laid eyes on him but hadn't acknowledged it until now.

Her avid gaze roved over his chest and down to where a line of dark hair dissected his tautly flat belly, down to the dark hair between his legs. Her mouth went dry when she saw his erection, long and thick and very hard. He brought a hand to himself, wrapping long fingers around the column of flesh as if to contain it…and it was the most erotic thing Charlotte had ever seen.

Her heart was thumping so loud she felt sure he must be able to hear it.

'Come here…'

She looked up, dizzy. He was watching her with a hunger that might have made her nervous if she'd had any brain cells left. She stepped closer and he took his hand off himself to reach for her, pulling her even closer so they touched. She could feel his arousal between them—insistent, hard.

He wrapped his arms around her and Charlotte lifted her arms to his neck, stretching up, relishing the friction of his chest against her breasts. Their mouths came together without hesitation, breath moving from one to the other as Salim angled her head so he could access her more fully.

When their tongues touched she made a groaning sound deep in her throat. He devoured her with a mastery that left her nowhere to hide, and she didn't want to hide. She revelled in the feel of his much bigger body next to hers, revelled in his strength. Revelled in the inherent differences between them.

His hands moved up and down her back, learning her shape. One hand cupped a buttock, squeezing gently. She pressed her thighs together to try and contain the rush of liquid heat. But it was impossible when that same hand explored back up her body, over her waist and in between them, finding the underside of her breast and cupping the plump weight.

He pulled back and looked down, and her gaze followed his to see her pale flesh cupped in his dark hand. He moved his thumb over her hard nipple and she bit her lip.

Suddenly the languorous energy between them seemed to change and thicken with something much more urgent and sharp.

'I want you, Charlotte...*now*.'

She looked up at him and gulped. She'd never seen

such an intense look on his face before. His bone structure stood out in stark relief. She nodded, her whole being saying *yes* to whatever he meant.

He took her hand and led her over to the bed, pulling her down with him onto the soft, decadent surface. As decadent as her behaviour. Salim raised himself over her and pulled her arms up so that they were over her head.

He looked at her. 'Stay like that.'

Charlotte didn't think she could move even if she wanted to. She was enslaved.

He watched her for a moment, as if she might disobey him, and she said roughly, 'I'm not moving.'

He smiled—brief and infinitely wicked. Then he looked his fill of her, his gaze slow and thorough.

The fact that she could fascinate Salim—a *king!*—on any level was terrifying and heady.

His hand moved over her, causing her stomach muscles to contract. He cupped her breast again, until it pouted wantonly towards his mouth, and when he bent his head and surrounded her tight nipple with heat and moisture she clasped her hands together over her head, so tightly it hurt. It was the only thing she could do to counteract the intense spiking of pleasure.

Her back arched helplessly towards him, and when he left one breast he ministered the same brand of torture to the other one, until Charlotte was flushed and panting, her whole body pulsating with need.

He lifted his head and looked at her, his expression feral. 'You're so responsive…why do you hide all this heat under that prim uniform, hmm?'

Charlotte had no coherent answer except the one in her head that was silent. *Because I hadn't met you yet…*

His hand drifted down again, over her belly and

lower, as he said throatily, 'Let's see how responsive you really are.'

He pushed her legs apart with gentle force, and every nerve in Charlotte's body seemed to migrate to between her legs in anticipation of his touch.

She still wasn't prepared when he did touch her, experimentally at first, on the very outside of where she ached most. Teasing her.

She couldn't keep her arms up any longer, and gripped his wide shoulders as he moved over her, his weight pressing down on her as that hand explored deeper between her legs. She gasped when his fingers slipped past the folds of aching flesh and released the liquid heat she'd been so desperately trying to contain.

He went still and muttered an Arabic curse, and for a second Charlotte felt acutely vulnerable. 'What's wrong?'

He shook his head and looked slightly stunned. 'Nothing... You... I had no idea a woman like you existed...'

As he spoke he slipped a finger inside her and Charlotte's thoughts scattered. She was too overcome to analyse what he'd just said or what it might mean.

She could feel her body resisting this intrusion, but as he explored her with a gentleness that belied the man she'd thought he was she felt her body softening, opening... One finger became two, and stretched her wider, going deeper, making the tension coiling deep within her snap and sharpen, searching for some kind of release.

She moved against his hand unconsciously, a little overwhelmed with all the sensations he was arousing. He bent his head and found her breast, licking her nipple back to stinging life before sucking it deep as his fingers still touched her intimately.

His mouth moved down her body, leaving a trail of hot kisses on her damp skin, and then his hand moved from between her legs. She immediately felt bereft—until his shoulders pushed her thighs even further apart.

She looked down and gasped. 'What are you—?'

'Shh... I need to taste you...to feel you on my tongue...' His words sounded slurred, as if he was drunk.

Too overwhelmed to do anything but submit, she felt him press kisses to her upper inner thighs, the scrape of his short beard sending shivers of sensation all over her body. When his mouth got closer to the very centre of her she went very still, her entire being thinking, *No...he won't...* But he did—with a thorough explicitness that made Charlotte's eyes roll back in her head.

His tongue licked right into the centre of her body and she couldn't breathe. Or think. Or move except to try and shy away from such an overload of pleasure. But his big hands were clamped on her thighs, holding her still, and then one hand moved under one buttock, gripping her firmly and lifting her so that he could explore her more fully.

Charlotte shuddered and gasped against Salim's mouth, and there was nothing to save her from the fall that came with shocking speed and force.

Her whole body was throbbing in the aftermath of an explosive orgasm. Salim moved up her body, and when she could open her eyes again she saw there was a distinctly smug look on his face.

He said roughly, 'You don't know how much I have wanted to see you undone like this...'

In a surprisingly tender move he brushed some hair

off her face. She could feel that it was damp, but she was too sated to care what she looked like. Her legs were spread in wanton abandonment and she could feel his body against hers. Hard. Needy.

Instinctively she reached for him, wanting to know how that stiff column of flesh would feel.

She wrapped her hand around him and saw how his facial muscles tightened, felt his whole body going still as she moved it experimentally up and down. His silky skin glided over the hard shaft of flesh and it fascinated her…its inherent strength and intense vulnerability.

Charlotte looked down and saw a bead of moisture. She spread it over the thick head of his erection but he stopped her hand with his.

She looked at him, suddenly unsure, and he said, 'If you keep doing that I'll spill right here…and I need to be inside you.'

Her heart stuttered as she watched him reach for protection and roll it onto his turgid flesh. He came over her, settling his hips between her legs, widening them further. Her muscles ached, but she barely noticed when she felt her body softening and ripening again.

He braced himself over her with a powerful arm, his other hand on his own body, guiding himself to her core… But when she expected him to thrust into her body instead he bent his head and kissed her, mimicking penetration with his tongue.

Charlotte moved against him, twining her arms around his neck, so that when he did thrust between her legs it was in tandem with his mouth and tongue and it stopped her gasp of shock and soothed it all at once.

He stopped moving for a moment, letting her body get used to his thickness, and she felt the resisting wall of muscle relax infinitesimally, allowing him to slide deeper. He did—with a groan that reverberated deep inside her.

For a moment it was too much—Charlotte felt impaled, and had an instinct to push him off her—but even as she put her hands to his shoulders and looked up at him the urge to push turned into something else. An urge to wrap her legs around him and keep him there.

His eyes burned down into hers and held her captive as he started to move in a relentless rhythm, in and out. Gradually Charlotte started to feel that urgency build again, and Salim slid an arm underneath her, arching her up towards him. He found her breast and sucked her nipple deep, and the twin sensations made her blood thunder under her skin.

Charlotte could feel the climax coming, but couldn't articulate any words to stop it for fear that she wasn't ready for it… On some dim level she knew she'd never be ready, and that all she could do was submit and let it sweep her away.

And that was exactly what it did. Salim's body moved within hers and she couldn't remember a time when she'd been a single entity.

Her body gave up its fight to resist the oncoming storm and shattered into a million pieces, her muscles milking him as he plunged deeper and deeper until he finally reached his own completion and her body claimed his, holding him deep within her as the final spasms of her own climax faded, until there was nothing left but the tattered remnants of the person she'd once been.

Salim knew the sandstorm had passed because there was a sense of stillness outside the tent and the sound of muffled of voices. No doubt the men were already in recovery mode in the early dawn—unearthing anything that had been buried during the storm.

That storm might have passed, but another one raged inside him. He was sitting in a chair on the opposite side of the tent from the bed, looking at the sleeping figure there warily, as if she might jump up at any moment and bite him.

He recalled her biting him last night, in the throes of her orgasm, on his shoulder. She'd broken his skin and he'd welcomed it.

Even now he couldn't really credit what had happened. The most intensely pleasurable sexual experience of his life. And the most vanilla. Sex with a virgin. You couldn't get more vanilla than that. And yet... Salim had felt like a novice too—learning his way into a woman's body for the first time.

She'd been a virgin.

The word resounded like an echoing klaxon: *virgin, virgin*.

He'd sensed it before he'd known for sure, and he knew that in any other situation, with any other woman, he would have run a mile at the merest suggestion of innocence. But it had only fired up his libido even more.

So her cooler than cool persona wasn't just a front. Unlocking her body had only made him think of all that she'd told him about her family and her upbringing. That sense of kinship echoed inside him again—they'd both suffered at the hands of their families and built up walls high enough to keep everyone out.

But after last night those walls were in danger of tumbling down around Salim's feet. And he could only imagine how seismic it had been for Charlotte to give up her innocence.

He'd wanted to bed her because he'd wanted her

more than he'd wanted any other woman and he'd na-
ively thought that would be enough. But he could feel
a clawing, raging hunger for *more*. Much more. And…
worse…he didn't just feel physical satisfaction. He'd
felt an elusive sense of peace steal over him in the moments just after his explosive orgasm, when his body
and Charlotte's had been joined so tightly that for a
second he hadn't wanted ever to break the connection.

What was he doing?

Salim stood up as adrenalin flooded his system—
the fight or flight impulse. He was an expert in letting
women know not to expect more than a no-strings encounter, and yet Charlotte—with her prim silk shirt
and pencil skirts and no fear of him—had burrowed
so far under his skin that he had all but forgotten his
own strict code of ethics. He'd wanted her that badly.

A very rare sense of disorientation made him feel
dizzy for a moment. He never lost sight of what was
important to him. And yet he was in danger of losing sight of a lot more. He was here in Tabat with one
aim—to promote and stabilise the country for someone
else to run—and yet that had been the last thing on his
mind over the past few days as he'd broken bread with
these tribes and had felt a mounting sense of owner-
ship take hold.

As if hearing his inner dialogue, Charlotte moved
on the bed and everything in Salim's body went still
and taut. Just then there was a noise from outside the
tent—a conspicuous clearing of a throat.

Salim tore his gaze from the still sleeping woman
on the bed and went to the entrance. He found Rafa
waiting for him.

'Sire, the storm wasn't as extensive as we feared so

we can leave this morning. But you need to speak with the elders before we go.'

Salim waited a beat and imagined Charlotte waking up, those green eyes landing on him, looking for something he wasn't prepared to give.

'Very well,' he said grimly, 'let's go.'

As he strode away from his tent he ignored the stinging of his conscience. He was just doing what he had done countless times before—walking away from a lover. This was no different and it couldn't afford to be—because he was in danger of forgetting why he was here at all.

Charlotte rose slowly through the levels of consciousness, registering aches and muscle twinges that told of a vigorous kind of activity she'd never indulged in before.

But the acute tenderness between her legs made her recall too easily and vividly what it had felt like to have Salim's powerful body thrusting deep inside hers, over and over again.

She opened her eyes with a snap, blinking in the dim light of the tent. The first thing she heard were voices from outside. The tent was empty, and when she came up on her elbows she saw her clothes laid out across the bottom of the bed.

Something curled up inside her.

What had she expected? To wake and find Salim mooning over her? Hadn't she gone to great pains to tell him she wasn't a romantic? That she just wanted dark and decadent things? And hadn't he obliged? *Thoroughly?*

She grabbed her clothes and went into the bathing area, washing quickly, avoiding her reflection in the mirror. When she re-emerged she felt a little disorientated in the empty tent. It was as if last night might have been a mirage, or a feverish erotic dream.

Suddenly Charlotte was terrified that Salim would appear before she was ready to see him, and she went to the opening of the tent, pulling back the flap of material. She saw sand piled against the surrounding tents, obviously shifted there by the storm, but it appeared not to have caused too much damage.

There was no one in the immediate vicinity and she escaped back to her own tent. When she got there she took a deep breath—but then almost jumped out of her skin when someone entered just behind her. She whirled around, her heart in her mouth. *Assa.* Her heart went back to a regular rhythm.

The girl looked distracted. 'Good—you're up, Miss McQuillan. The storm wasn't as bad as they feared, so we'll leave for Tabat City shortly. You should gather your things. The king is eager to be back before sunset.'

I bet he is, thought Charlotte, ignoring the dart of hurt that he didn't seem to be overly concerned as to her wellbeing this morning.

She got her things together and packed. The fact that he hadn't been there when she'd woken, hadn't thought to wake her, told her in no uncertain terms that she was most likely already consigned to the box where he stored regretful experiences. If the man had any regrets—which he probably didn't.

By the time the staff were loading up the vehicles Charlotte could see Salim in the distance, tall and dominant. He was speaking to the sheikh of the tribe, and then he got into his SUV and it took off ahead of the convoy, flanked by Security in their four by fours.

Rafa appeared, and to Charlotte's over-sensitive mind it seemed he looked at her with an expression of pity.

'You will travel with me, Miss McQuillan.'

She forced a smile, as if this was totally fine, and told herself that she wasn't devastated by the way Salim obviously couldn't bear to look at her. The thought that this genteel older gentleman might know what had happened was nearly too much to bear.

As they drove across the undulating desert, getting closer and closer to civilisation again, Salim's morning-after treatment of Charlotte continued to grate on her exposed nerves, even though she knew it shouldn't.

She cursed herself for having believed that something revelatory had happened last night. It had been sex. Her first sexual experience, yes. But just sex. The fact that Salim hadn't appeared even to notice that he'd been her first lover was something she shouldn't be disappointed by. After all, she'd hoped that he wouldn't notice. But the fact that he *hadn't* wasn't as easy to live with as she'd thought.

And, worse, it stung her where she was most vulnerable—where her parents had left an indelible mark of rejection and abandonment. *This* was what she'd wanted to protect herself from, and to think that she'd allowed someone close enough to rip those wounds open again was as humiliating as it was painful.

She'd deluded herself last night, thinking she could take what Salim offered and remain untouched. She'd wanted him badly enough to lie to herself.

They reached the palace in Tabat City as the sun was setting over the ancient building, bathing everything with a lush golden light, but Charlotte was oblivious to the beauty, her guts churning.

She got out of the car and stretched her cramped legs. She saw Salim in the distance, dark shades covering his eyes. He looked in her direction briefly, but then turned and strode into the palace with his retinue following behind him. He'd never looked more king-like than at that moment.

Assa appeared at Charlotte's side. 'I will draw you a bath, Miss McQuillan, and have some food brought to your room. You must be tired.'

Tired, hot and dusty. And still aching in secret places.

She followed Assa back to her room but a couple of hours later, after food and a bath, Charlotte couldn't settle.

She'd half expected—*hoped*—to see Salim appear, but since the sun had set and night had fallen over the desert outside there'd been no visitors. She felt power-less, and it was far too reminiscent of when she'd been younger, when she'd been at the mercy of her parents' whims.

She hated to think that after all she'd been through she had allowed herself to be treated so cavalierly, that somewhere in this vast crumbling palace Salim was oblivious to her turmoil.

And she hated it that she couldn't stop thinking about the fact that he was proving to be far more complex than she'd ever have given him credit for: the king who was too selfish to rule his own people and yet had conducted himself like a king for the past week.

He hadn't made love to her like a reprobate playboy last night. He'd made love to her like a man who cared more for her pleasure than his own. And yet today he'd treated her as if she didn't exist.

Nothing added up.

Galvanised by something deep inside that wouldn't rest, Charlotte changed out of the robe she wore and into plain trousers and the loose tribal shirt she'd bought from the women of the Jadar tribe. She looked at herself quickly in the mirror and grimaced at her tousled hair, but left it as it was. She couldn't remember the last time it had been sleek and neat.

Before she could stop and rationalise what she was doing, Charlotte slipped out of her room and along the long corridor that led up to Salim's private quarters. She only noticed halfway there that she was in bare feet, but didn't stop.

The palace was silent, and it was only when she reached Salim's door that she faltered. A bodyguard stood outside, but he recognised her and said in Arabic, 'Good evening, Miss McQuillan. You have a meeting with King Al-Noury?'

She nodded, crossing her fingers at the white lie.

He opened the door and let her go inside. Charlotte hadn't been to Salim's quarters before, and saw that it was a vast labyrinth of rooms. The decor was masculine and heavy. Dark. Perhaps these had been his grandfather's rooms.

She walked through the nearest door and found herself in a huge living area, with low couches dotted around coffee tables and a media centre in one corner where world news played on mute in the background.

And then her gaze landed on the tall figure standing by one of the windows. Her heart palpitated. He moved out of the shadows and into the low light of the room. His bone structure looked even more austere. He wore a white shirt and black trousers, once more the urbane Western billionaire. Albeit still with the beard and sexily messy hair.

For a second a sense of *déjà-vu* hit her as she recalled what that beard had felt like tickling her tender inner thighs. Charlotte wondered a little desperately if a man like Salim could ever be tamed?

He was holding a bulbous crystal glass in one hand and he raised it towards her, the amber liquid catching the light. 'Can I offer you a drink?'

Charlotte swallowed the dryness in her mouth. She shook her head. The last thing she needed was anything that made her feel dizzier.

'Was there something you wanted, Charlotte?'

He sounded almost bored, and not remotely surprised to see her. As if he'd been waiting for her because he knew she wouldn't be able to resist coming to him.

She cursed herself for having ever thought there might be hidden depths to him and felt her emotions bubble over.

She clenched her hands into fists at her sides. 'It's true what they say—you really are a bastard, aren't you?'

CHAPTER SEVEN

A SENSE OF *déjà-vu* hit Salim like a punch to his gut. The words she'd just uttered were words he was well used to hearing from women, but none had scored along his insides like a serrated knife before.

When he'd turned around just now, to see Charlotte standing just a few feet away, for a second he'd thought that he'd conjured her up out of the desire that was clawing at his insides, making a mockery of his determination to relegate her to a one-night aberration.

Salim couldn't stop his gaze dipping hungrily to the vee neck of the tribal shirt and the way it clung to her breasts. The material was so fine he could see she wore no bra, and his body responded forcibly to the memory of how those firm swells had felt in his hands. How they'd felt pressed against his chest as she'd arched into him. How they'd tasted under his tongue.

She *was* real, and he felt exposed.

Irritation at her ability to slide under his skin so effortlessly made him ask curtly, 'Why didn't you tell me you were a virgin?'

She blanched slightly, some of her bravado slipping. 'So you did notice?'

Salim felt grim. 'I may be a bastard but I'm also an

experienced lover, and last night was your first time, wasn't it?'

Charlotte didn't shy away from his question. She stepped forward and looked him directly in the eye. 'Yes, it was.'

As direct and forthright as ever. No games there.

'Then why me? Why now?'

Do you really want to know the answer to that? asked a voice. But it was too late.

Colour flared along her cheeks. 'Because you're the first man I've ever wanted like that. It was sex, pure and simple, Salim. Nothing more.'

He looked at her for a long moment, as if he could convince himself of the veracity of her words. They should be making him feel better, but if anything they only compounded his conflicting emotions because he doubted it was that pure and simple at all.

He felt compelled to goad her. 'When I lost my virginity I believed myself in love… For about a week, until I found my lover in bed with one of my security detail.'

Her eyes sparked at that, and she stepped forward. 'So that's why you weren't there when I woke this morning—to make sure I didn't get any ideas.'

Salim's conscience pricked hard. 'I don't *do* cosy mornings after.'

Charlotte folded her arms and it pushed the swells of her breasts up beneath the flimsy material of her shirt. Salim gritted his jaw.

'Believe me, I didn't imagine for a second that you did. I'm not in love with you, Salim, and I wasn't looking to wake up in your arms. But a little acknowledgement of what we'd shared might have been nice.'

Honesty forced him to admit, 'You deserved for your first time to be with a better man than me.'

Charlotte was stunned. The very thought of not having had that experience with this man made her go cold inside. No man would ever make her feel like that again. She knew that with fatal certainty.

She let her arms drop to her sides. 'But I wanted *you*.'

Salim's hand tightened on the glass he held. 'Because I gave you little choice. I suspected your innocence but I seduced you anyway.'

Charlotte shook her head. 'I know my own mind, Salim. I made the choice—you asked me if I was sure, don't you remember?'

'Did I?'

She nodded. 'Why would you think you're not worthy?'

His mouth tightened. He was looking at her, but not seeing her. He'd gone somewhere else.

'I've gone after what I want for so long that it's second nature for me to disregard others' opinions. That's why I won't remain as King of Tabat. If anything, this past week has proved to me even more that they deserve someone better.'

Charlotte struggled to process this. 'What are you talking about?'

Salim's gaze narrowed on hers, and for the first time she saw something raw and unguarded in those blue depths. Raw enough to make her suck in a breath.

He said, 'I've lived my life with two main objectives: to distance myself from my inheritance and family and to avenge my sister's death.'

Charlotte's chest tightened. 'Why did you have to avenge it?'

Salim made a curt gesture with his hand. 'That's not important now. What is important is that I know my limitations, and I am not prepared to be king. I haven't spent hours studying, like my brother. I've lived my life in a way that should convince people that I'm not remotely suitable. And yet they don't seem to want to accept that.'

'Because,' Charlotte said quietly, 'they see what I saw this week—a man prepared to sit down and learn about his country. You didn't need me there at all. Your destiny—whether you like to admit it or not—is in your DNA. You're a king, Salim, and your people can see that.'

There was no disguising the bleakness she saw in his eyes now. This was no playboy. This was a tortured man.

'Would you say the same if you knew I'd driven a man to his death in the name of vengeance?'

Her breath stopped. 'What do you mean?'

'I took a life for a life.'

Charlotte knew he must be talking about his sister. 'But you didn't actually…kill someone?'

He let out a short harsh laugh. 'Not with my hands, but as good as.'

Charlotte knew instinctively that whatever had happened Salim wasn't responsible in the way he obviously believed. But she guessed he wouldn't elaborate, or appreciate hearing her thoughts.

She could also see very clearly that his motives for not wanting to be King of Tabat for longer than absolutely necessary had nothing to do with his own selfish needs. It was based on something far deeper and darker.

Acting on an instinct she couldn't deny, Charlotte reached out and took the glass of alcohol out of Salim's hand. She raised it to her mouth and drained it. The liquid slid down her throat, leaving a burning fire in its wake and rushing to her head.

She put the glass down carefully on a table and looked back up at Salim. He was watching her. Emotion surged in spite of her best efforts to burn it away with the whisky.

She aimed for a wry smile, but it felt wobbly. 'You don't actually need my expertise at all—you're a natural.'

'Are you telling me you think your services are no longer required?' Salim's voice was harsh.

The rush of alcohol-induced confidence trickled away and Charlotte felt cold. 'No…that's not what I'm saying.'

'So what are you saying?'

She refused to let this austere Salim scare her away. 'Do you want me, Salim? Because if you don't that's fine. I'll leave right now.'

For a heart-stopping moment she saw the struggle on his face and in his eyes.

But then he reached for her as he said gutturally, 'Yes, damn you—yes, I want you.'

It was all she needed to hear. She reached up and put her arms around his neck, pressed her mouth to his.

Salim knew he was playing with fire, but he was incapable of resisting. Charlotte's mouth moved under his and he gave in to the dark hunger inside him—a voracious, needy hunger.

He wrapped his arms around her back and hauled her to him, feeling the length of her slender body trembling against his as he took control of the kiss and gorged on the sweetness she was offering.

Charlotte gave up trying to make any sense of anything—she just knew, as Salim started kissing her back, clearly showing her who was boss in this exchange, that she never wanted him to stop.

He'd awakened her on a sexual level but she knew very well that their time was finite. She felt that same greedy desire she had last night, to experience as much as she could.

When he pulled back from kissing her she went with him, opening her eyes, her vision blurry for a minute. He took her by the hand and led her through his rooms and into a vast bedroom, dominated by the biggest bed she'd ever seen in her life.

He stopped by the bed and let her hand go. 'I want to see you.'

Charlotte's inhibitions had been burnt away by alcohol and revelations. She had nothing left to hide behind, so she took off her clothes.

Salim's blue gaze devoured her from head to toe. Once again the thought that he could find her so compelling was unbelievable and heady. Too heady to resist.

He reached for her and pulled her close. Her hands automatically searched for his shirt buttons, undoing them unsteadily because he was pushing her hair back and pressing kisses to her neck and shoulder, the scratch of his beard sending shivers through her whole body.

Her breasts felt heavy as he cupped one in his hand, his thumb moving back and forth over her nipple. The sensations connected directly to the pulse between her legs, where she was throbbing with hot, damp need.

When he pulled back slightly his shirt was open, but still tucked in. He made short work of untucking it and pulling it off, his hands going to his belt and then his trousers, undoing them and pushing them down to the floor.

Now he wore just briefs, and they were tented over his erection. Charlotte remembered how she had felt when he'd thrust inside her…how full and stretched… She reached out instinctively and cupped a hand over him.

He said roughly, 'Take them off.'

With trembling hands she pulled them down from his lean hips and over his erection, down over powerful thighs and to the floor. She was almost kneeling at his feet now, and she stayed there.

She looked at that part of him that was so unashamedly masculine. She reached out and heard the breath hiss through his teeth as she wrapped her hand around his length, fascinated by the silky smoothness of the skin around that column of steel arising out of dark hair.

She touched the bead of moisture at its head with her thumb. She wanted to taste it and leant forward, licking with her tongue. Lust exploded inside her as the tart, salty taste impacted on her tastebuds and she wanted to taste more. She placed her mouth around him and for a heady moment felt a sense of unbelievable feminine power as she explored the bulbous head of his erection with her mouth and tongue.

But then he stepped back, out of her reach, and his hands came under her arms, lifting her up.

She immediately felt self-conscious. 'Was I doing something wrong?'

Salim shook his head, his eyes burning so bright it almost hurt to look into them. 'No. But I need to be inside you right now more than I need your mouth on me…'

'Oh…'

Her heart thumped hard as Salim took her to the bed and she lay down. He came down beside her, all bronzed skin and rippling muscles. He put a hand on her thighs, opening them, and then placed his hand on the beating heart of her body before stroking her damp folds with his finger. She had to bite back a moan, she was so acutely sensitised.

Salim pressed his mouth to hers, his tongue tasting her explicitly before he drew back and said, 'Let it out... I want to hear you...'

As if to make her moan out loud, one finger became two and he thrust them in and out. The ache deep inside her grew tight and sharp. It was even sharper when his mouth encircled one breast and he drew her hard nipple in deep, suckling at the tingling flesh until she couldn't hold back any longer and moaned a plea into his shoulder...

Charlotte couldn't breathe. She was caught in a spiral of growing need. Blindly she searched for and found Salim's hard flesh, wrapping a hand around him, stroking up and down in an instinctive rhythm. She revelled in the way his breath hissed between his teeth and his muscles went taut.

He moved over her, dominating her easily...but in a way that made her excitement increase.

She explored with more confidence now, her hand still caressing him as she kissed his shoulder and moved her mouth down, exploring a hard nipple and administering the same torture he'd inflicted on her.

Salim reached to the side of the bed for something and donned protection. She moved so that she was under him, and his body settled between her spread legs as if this was a dance they'd done many times before. If she could think more clearly it would been scary how *right* this felt...

In silent answer to the question he hadn't even asked,

she just tilted her hips up towards him so that the blunt head of his erection was notched right against her body, a mere breath away from—

Aahhh...

She moaned as he slid in slowly, watching her face. She was surrounded by heat and sensation, but he was going too slowly, so she wrapped her legs around his waist and dug her heels into his muscular buttocks.

He huffed out a laugh and gave in to her body's demands, thrusting so deep inside her that for a long moment she couldn't breathe. And then he started to move, and her breath came back, and she was soaring, flying higher and higher, until everything went still inside her. It felt like a tiny death—and then she exploded back into life and crashed and burned...

Salim couldn't hold back a guttural curse as the powerful inner muscles of Charlotte's body drew him in so thoroughly that he couldn't keep from falling over the edge behind her.

It had been fast and furious. He'd never felt less in control of his own body. They'd touched and ignited immediately. He'd never experienced anything like it before.

It seemed to take for ever for his heart to slow down again as he lay slumped over Charlotte's body. Her legs had fallen to his sides and he could feel the aftershock ripples of her inner muscles along his length, keeping him hard.

He lifted his head and looked down. She opened her eyes slowly and something turned over in his chest. Her cheeks were flushed and her lips were swollen. Damp strands of strawberry-golden hair were stuck to her cheek. He tucked it back.

She looked as shocked as he felt—as if they'd both got caught in a sudden earthquake.

And then he became aware of his weight on her and reluctantly moved off her, going into the bathroom to take care of the protection.

He looked at himself for a moment in the mirror and felt a sense of *déjà-vu* as he recalled when he'd looked at himself a few weeks ago, just before talking with his brother Zafir. He'd felt jaded then—weary. Hollow.

Now he felt none of those things.

He felt as if he was connected to something much bigger than himself. Something just out of sight, intangible but solid.

Destiny, whispered a voice.

Salim scowled at his reflection—it was not destiny. It was just post-great-sex endorphins. His life wasn't changing—not for anything, and certainly not for great sex or because he'd found himself feeling more at home in Tabat than anywhere else he'd been in his life.

He heard a faint noise from the bedroom and went back to find Charlotte sitting on the edge of the bed, looking at him over her shoulder. Her naked back was delicate and pale, and just like that his body started coming back to life.

Her gaze dropped and widened as she took him in.

He strolled back to the bed and asked, with a bite that reflected his unwelcome post-coital thoughts, 'Were you going somewhere?'

He got onto the bed and reached for her, pulling her back towards him until she went off-balance and landed on her back.

She looked up at him, a slight wariness on her face, as if she could sense his volatile mood. 'I'm going back to my room.'

Salim smiled, and felt ruthless when he said, 'Wrong answer.'

And then he drowned out the myriad voices in his head by losing himself in her all over again.

When Charlotte woke the following morning she was relieved to find herself alone in Salim's bed. She couldn't have handled being under the scrutiny of that searing blue gaze when she felt so turned inside out.

Last night was almost too much to process. The mind-melting sex…and the revelations that had preceded it.

Salim didn't believe he was worthy of his kingdom.

He'd led her to believe that he didn't want to be king because he didn't want to give up his successful independent lifestyle. But it was so much more than that. Not to mention the fact that he believed he'd driven someone to his death.

Charlotte didn't for a second believe that was true. But *he* did.

She heard a noise and sat up in the bed in a panic, pulling the sheet up to her neck, not remotely ready to face Salim.

But it was Assa, and relief vied with embarrassment as the young girl came in, seemingly totally unfazed to find Charlotte in her king's bed.

'Miss McQuillan, the king will be leaving for Jandor soon. I've packed your bags and laid out some clothes in your room.'

Assa handed her a robe and Charlotte squeaked out, 'Jandor?'

The girl nodded. 'Yes, for the banquet dinner King Zafir is holding in Jahor palace, in honour of our king's upcoming coronation.' Assa's eyes shone with excitement as she said, 'I can't wait to see Queen Kat—they say she's even more beautiful than in her pictures.'

Charlotte smiled weakly and pulled the robe on. Of course. She'd completely forgotten about the scheduled trip to Jandor in the tumult of the past few days.

She followed Assa back to her rooms through a warren of back corridors—presumably to protect Charlotte's sullied reputation.

She tried to stop herself wondering where Salim was, or if he was even marginally as affected as she was by the previous night.

Salim was already on his private jet when she stepped on board a few hours later. He looked up and there was no discernible expression on his face. Charlotte tried not to let that intimidate her, or to feel out of her depth. She had so little experience with this kind of thing.

When she took a seat on the other side of the aisle, directed there by a steward, she realised that Salim was listening to Rafa, who was sitting opposite him and had been hidden by the seat.

Salim stared at her, and his gaze drifted down over her silk shirt and plain trousers. When he met her eyes again he arched a brow.

She'd found herself choosing from her own clothes again, even though Assa had left out a traditional tunic, because at the last minute she'd felt as if she needed some fortification. Except now all she could think was that she'd dressed like this subconsciously to provoke a reaction, and she cringed inwardly.

Rafa stood up then, collecting a sheaf of papers, and bowed to Salim before smiling at Charlotte and taking his leave.

She asked, 'Isn't he travelling with us?'

The staff were busy closing the door as Salim said, 'He's travelling separately.'

He came out of his seat then, and was buckling her belt across her lap before she could move. His hands were big against her belly as he tightened it.

He looked at her and said, *sotto voce*, 'Did you dress like that on purpose, Charlotte?'

A wave of heat scorched her insides, all the way to between her legs. She felt a spurt of something giddy and reckless. 'Maybe I did.'

His eyes flashed and his hands lingered for a moment before the plane started moving on the runway and he took his seat again.

When they were airborne, and the staff had checked if they needed anything, Salim undid his belt and held out a hand to Charlotte across the aisle.

'Come here,' he instructed.

Charlotte glanced up the plane to where the steward was keeping himself discreetly busy. She looked back at Salim and melted inside. The look on his face was one of such innate imperiousness that she couldn't understand how he didn't see it in himself.

Undoing her belt, she stood up and felt ridiculously shy. Salim took her hand in his and tugged her towards him until she all but fell into his lap.

'Salim!' she hissed, mindful of the staff.

He just smiled wickedly as he curved her body into his much harder one. Charlotte felt hot and breathless and exhilarated. His hands were in her hair, undoing the smooth chignon that Assa had created with such assiduousness earlier.

'Salim…' She trailed off weakly as her hair fell down and he ran his hands through it, mussing it up. She'd already gathered that he liked to muss her up as much as possible.

'Why do you do it?' His voice rumbled against her breasts, which were pressed against his chest.

'Do what?' she asked, feeling dizzy.

His hand was on her back now, shaping her body under her silk shirt, finding where it was tucked into her trousers and sliding underneath to find bare skin.

'Hide your true nature.'

Instantly Charlotte was tense. Her true nature was to seek order in a chaotic world by any means necessary, and to erect a façade that was becoming increasingly flimsy.

'What do you mean?' she asked warily.

He looked at her. 'You're a deeply passionate and sensual woman, Charlotte. Yet you hide behind these prim suits. You revelled in the freedom of the desert—you appreciated it in a way that most Western people would never understand. It called to something in you.'

Charlotte felt as if someone had pushed her off a cliff and she was free-falling. How was it that this man could see so much? She'd never thought of herself as passionate before...not until now. Until him. And, as for the desert, she did feel a deep affinity for it and she had no idea where it had come from.

Salim was looking at her.

She shrugged lightly, not really wanting to talk about this but unable to escape. 'I always saw passion as something selfish...showy. Fickle. My parents were passionate, and then suddenly they weren't. They detested each other.' She avoided Salim's eye, focusing on his shoulder. 'I never trusted it, or wanted to be like them.'

Salim touched a finger to her chin, forcing her to look at him. 'Well, it's too late for that. You have it in spades. Passion and sensuality. I'm amazed you've lasted this long without letting anyone see that.'

A sharp poignancy filled Charlotte then, as she wondered what might have happened if she'd never met Salim. Would she have lived her life never knowing the true depth of pleasure a man could give a woman? Never knowing the true depth of her own nature?

She said a little shakily, 'I could say the same to you. You're a far less selfish man than you'd have others believe. I think Tabat has called to you, whether you like it or not, and you can't simply go back to your life…'

She felt the tension in Salim's body as he reacted to that, but Charlotte knew she was right. He didn't like it, though. She saw the shutters come down over his expression and his eyes glittered.

'Don't let lust infuse everything—including me—with a rose-coloured glow. I'm still the same, and I want the same things. This…what's between us…will burn out. It always does.'

Charlotte felt a mix of hurt and anger. She tensed and pushed herself away from Salim as much as he would allow. 'You don't need to patronise me, I might have been a virgin, but I'm not completely innocent. I do know how these things work. My rose-tinted glasses got broken a long time ago.'

Tension simmered between them for a second, and then it changed into something hotter. The muscles in Salim's face relaxed and his hand started wandering again, sliding up her bare back under her shirt, finding the clasp of her bra and undoing it expertly before she had a chance to stop him.

And it was too late. Her blood was boiling with lust now, and not anger.

He pressed a kiss to her jaw and said, 'Good. We both know where we stand, then.'

As his wicked mouth and hands robbed her all too easily of speech and rational thought Charlotte wondered a little hysterically what she'd just agreed to—because it felt very much as if she'd just given Salim licence to toy with her for as long as it suited him.

And as for her confident assertion that her rose-tinted glasses had been broken long ago—that felt dangerously hollow now.

CHAPTER EIGHT

BY THE TIME they'd landed, and Charlotte was walking down the steps of the plane and into the blazing Jandor sunshine, she felt thoroughly mussed and extremely ill-prepared.

Just moments ago, when Charlotte had seen the car outside bearing the king's flag, she'd rounded on Salim, feeling prickly and off-centre. She'd frantically tried to repair the damage done to her clothes, hair and make-up.

'You should have warned me your brother and his wife were coming to meet us. What on earth will they think? I haven't even briefed myself on everything I need to know about them and Jandor.'

For someone who'd always prided herself on her professional decorum, she'd felt very exposed.

Salim had just looked at her with a small smile playing around his mouth. 'Charlotte, please don't take this as a criticism of your ability, which is commendable, but even you would have to admit that your professional services haven't exactly been exercised for the past couple of weeks.'

'No,' she said hotly, tucking her hair up as best she could, acutely aware of the royal entourage lining up outside the plane. 'Because for one thing you wouldn't let me do my job, and for another you proved to be far more of a natural diplomat than you'd ever like to admit.'

And distracting!

If she'd hoped to provoke a reaction it hadn't worked. Salim had just coolly stood up and watched as she'd tucked herself in.

Now, a man who was undoubtedly Salim's brother stood with a stunningly beautiful woman at the bottom of the steps.

King Zafir was of the same height and build as Salim, but where Salim's eyes were blue Zafir's were dark grey and deep-set. He had a more austere demeanour than Salim, and she could feel the tension snap between the two men as they greeted one another with the traditional clasping of the shoulders.

Queen Kat had been one of the world's most famous supermodels until she'd disappeared off the scene almost two years before. It had since transpired that she'd suffered a cataclysmic trauma when she'd been involved in an accident and had had to have her lower left leg amputated.

Not that you would know it now, as she stood tall and regal beside her husband, with a warm but concerned look in her mesmerising golden eyes as she took in the exchange between the brothers.

Then King Zafir put out his hand towards Charlotte. 'Miss McQuillan, it's a pleasure to finally meet you, and it's even more of a pleasure to see that my brother has availed himself of your considerable services and professionalism.'

Charlotte felt her face get mortifyingly hot. She sensed Salim's mocking look in her direction and took

King Zafir's hand, willing down the heat. 'It's lovely to meet you too. Call me Charlotte, please.'

Queen Kat stepped forward then, and Charlotte couldn't help but be dazzled by her beauty and the very obviously happy glow of the recently married couple.

'Charlotte, how lovely to meet you—welcome to Jahor.'

Her smile was genuine and Charlotte couldn't fail to respond in kind.

Charlotte noticed that Salim greeted his new sister-in-law with polite civility, but not much warmth. It didn't take a clairvoyant to sense that he wanted to be anywhere but here. It had been evident from his growing tension on the plane as soon as they'd entered Jandor airspace.

He said now, to his brother, 'You really didn't need to come all the way out here to meet us.'

King Zafir's jaw tightened and Charlotte felt breathless for a second at how similar the men were.

'I haven't seen you since our father's funeral. A trip to greet you at the airport was not a chore, brother.'

Salim flushed. He obviously knew he was being rude, and Charlotte had an instinct to put her hand into his, offering silent support but of course she couldn't.

Queen Kat took her by the arm. 'Come on, let's go to the palace. I'm sure you could do with some refreshment.'

Charlotte smiled and let herself be led away to the first in a fleet of cars. It appeared that she was to travel with Kat and that the brothers would travel together in the car behind. She saw that King Zafir had got into the driver's seat and Salim into the passenger one, looking stony-faced. Charlotte wondered why there was such a schism between them—surely their adverse relationship with their parents should have bonded them?

Kat chatted easily in the back of their car, and Charlotte found herself relaxing as they wound their way up the narrow streets to the palace.

She said shyly, 'Congratulations on your wedding.'

Kat smiled radiantly. 'Thank you. Sometimes I still can't believe it myself. My life has changed so utterly, and I won't lie and say that becoming queen doesn't intimidate me every day!' She scrunched up her nose. 'But, not wanting to sound too corny about it, with Zafir by my side I feel capable of pretty much anything. I just want to make him proud—and Jandor.'

It shook Charlotte to see this evidence of their loving bond up close, and she didn't think it was just newly wedded bliss. From what she recalled, the couple had been together before, but had split up before Kat's catastrophic accident and had since reunited. A little dart of what felt like envy gripped her down low in her belly, at the sight of such devotion.

They were pulling into the palace forecourt now, and Kat put a hand on Charlotte's arm, saying with a pointed look at her blouse, 'You might want to redo your buttons before we get out.'

Charlotte looked down and gasped when she realised her shirt buttons were done up haphazardly. She rectified the situation with a flaming face, and vowed silently to kill Salim for not warning her. But then she caught Kat's eye again, and saw that the woman had a sympathetic but amused look on her face.

'Don't worry, it's not that obvious. But I do know what it's like to fall for an Al-Noury man.'

Charlotte shook her head, and opened her mouth to deny it automatically—but then shut it again when words wouldn't come. A feeling of dread mixed with exhilaration infused her whole body. And a very stark revelation. She *was* falling for Salim.

It took her a second to focus on the woman looking at her so sympathetically, as if she knew exactly what had just gone through Charlotte's head.

Stunned and feeling winded, Charlotte asked, 'Is it that obvious?'

Kat's smile was knowing. 'What you were getting up to on the plane? Yes. But as for anything deeper—it's only obvious to me because your expression reminds me of how I feel when I look at my own husband.'

Someone was opening Charlotte's door now, and she took the opportunity to escape from Kat's sympathetic golden gaze.

When she was out of the car, the awe-inspiring golden magnificence of the Jahor palace distracted her from what had just transpired.

The place was a hive of activity as Kat walked her through the ornate entrance, saying, 'I know Zafir wants to talk business with Salim, so I thought we could take refreshments in the garden?'

'Please don't feel you have to entertain me,' Charlotte said quickly, acutely aware that Kat must be busy with the banquet that evening. And more acutely feeling a need to go somewhere private and quiet, where she could assimilate what had just happened.

But the queen said, with her soft American twang, 'Honestly, you'll be doing me a favour. I'm shamelessly using you as a decoy to get them to talk while they can. And I won't bring up what we just spoke of unless you do.'

Charlotte admitted defeat in the face of Kat's easy warmth and charm. She'd never been a girly girl, but for the first time she could imagine that she would like a woman like Kat as a friend.

She smiled. 'If you're sure I'm not putting you out?'

Kat took her arm again and shepherded her through the palace, past vast corridors and beautiful courtyard gardens. 'I'm sure. Now, I want to hear all about what it is exactly that you do, because it sounds totally fascinating...'

About an hour later Charlotte was even more impressed with Kat. She knew the woman was an amputee, but apart from a small but definite limp it was impossible to tell—especially when her cream and gold kaftan effectively hid any sign of a prosthetic leg.

Kat was showing her the gardens after a delicious tea, and Charlotte stopped when she saw the entrance into a walled garden where a fountain of water burbled into an exquisite pool and wild exotic flowers bloomed in every corner.

Unable to stop herself, she walked to the entrance and looked in. Kat came alongside her and Charlotte said, 'It's beautiful...so peaceful.'

Kat grimaced and stepped into the garden. Charlotte followed.

'It wasn't always like this. It was an abandoned ruin for many years...'

'Why?'

But before Kat could respond another voice, unmistakably male and familiar, cut in harshly.

'Because it shouldn't have been touched, that's why. Who the hell is responsible for this?'

Charlotte whirled around at the sudden arrival of Salim. 'Where did you come from?'

He flicked a glance at Charlotte, and she was shocked at the depth of cold anger in his eyes.

'I was looking for you.'

Queen Kat was contrite. 'Salim, I thought I was doing a good thing. I know this is where—'

He cut her off. 'You know nothing. You shouldn't have done this. You had no right.'

He'd turned and strode out of the garden again before Charlotte could take in what had just happened, his long robe billowing after him. She looked at Kat, who was obviously upset, and anger swelled at his unforgivable treatment of his sister-in-law.

Charlotte said, 'I'm so sorry, Kat, you didn't deserve that at all. I'll go after him.'

The other woman caught her hand and said, 'Please tell him I'm sorry. I thought I was doing a good thing in her memory…'

Salim knew that he had just behaved unforgivably. Charlotte's look of shock was etched into his brain. As was Kat's contrite response. His sister-in-law didn't deserve his opprobrium—but seeing what she'd done to that place had cracked something open inside him. Something raw.

Being back here was fraught enough with painful memories and reminders of how he'd turned his back on so much…on his brother—

'Salim!'

Charlotte.

Her voice stopped his self-recrimination and was like balm to a wound. As that registered fully Salim suddenly resented the fact that she'd slid so far under his skin. That she'd witnessed that moment.

He stopped and whirled around on the path to see Charlotte hurrying towards him. She stopped, her chest moving up and down enticingly under that silk blouse. She was angry.

'What on earth is wrong with you, speaking to Kat like that?'

Salim lashed out. 'I'm sorry—was that not very diplomatic? Is Queen Kat your new best friend? Perhaps you like what you see and you're fancying your chances of becoming a queen, too?'

Charlotte's face leached of colour and her green eyes stood out starkly against her pale skin. Salim felt immediate remorse.

Before she could respond he said roughly, 'I'm sorry. That was unforgivable. You didn't deserve that, and Kat didn't deserve it either.'

Still looking a little shaken, Charlotte said, 'Then why? What is that place?'

Salim looked up into the sky for a moment, drawing in a long breath, and then looked back down. 'It's where Sara died. She was on the high wall and she fell. She had a massive head injury…she died in my arms.'

Charlotte started towards him. 'Oh, Salim…'

But he held out his hand, stopping her. If she touched him he wasn't sure he wouldn't shatter completely.

She shook her head, eyes bright with an emotion that caught at Salim's chest, making it tight.

'What a tragic accident.'

Salim steeled himself. He didn't have to tell her. He didn't have to say a word. But he couldn't stop it spilling out, as if some force was compelling him.

'That's just it—it wasn't an accident. She fell off that wall deliberately. She didn't want to die but she did.' His voice had turned unbearably harsh.

Charlotte frowned, clearly not understanding. She looked so pale that Salim went over to her, taking her arm and making her sit down on a nearby stone bench.

She looked up at him. 'What are you talking about?'

Salim paced back and forth, cursing himself for having given in to the impulse to unburden himself while at the same time feeling a sense of compulsion to keep going. As if he knew this was the only way the heavy weight he bore might ever be lightened.

He stopped in front of Charlotte.

'Sara and I were always joined at the hip. We were so close we even had our own language. One week, not long after our eleventh birthday, our father was hosting an economic forum. Ambassadors from neighbouring countries were here, as well as representatives from all over the world. It was a big, prestigious event. Sara had been tasked to do some things with our mother, to help out, so we were separated during the week. I didn't notice until almost the end of the week that something was wrong. Sara was avoiding me...not talking.'

Charlotte asked quietly, 'What happened?'

'I was in the walled garden—it was our favourite place to hide and play. She came in and I knew something was wrong. I'd never seen her so subdued... Eventually she told me—' He stopped.

Charlotte stood up. 'Go on.'

Salim's jaw was tight, constricting his voice. 'It was the Italian ambassador. An oily, sleazy man. He'd taken a liking to Sara and had persuaded my mother to let her attend to him especially.'

Charlotte put a hand to her mouth, clearly jumping to a dark conclusion.

Salim continued. 'Up to that point he hadn't actually touched her, but he'd said something to scare her enough to take her clothes off, telling her he just wanted to look at her. When she told me this she couldn't even look at me. She was so ashamed. She told me how he'd kept telling her she was perfect, and that before he left he would show her how a man kissed a woman…how they touched each other…'

'Oh, Salim…'

But Salim didn't hear Charlotte's voice. He was back in that garden, his insides turning to jelly as he watched his sister—his life—transform into someone he didn't know. Someone haunted and terrified. Someone who had lost her innocence.

She'd climbed up onto the high wall in spite of his pleas and said through her tears.

I don't want him to look at me again, and if I'm not perfect, he won't like me anymore…'

Salim's voice was toneless. 'She jumped off the wall deliberately, to try and injure herself enough so that she would no longer draw the eye of a debased man. She believed this because when our older brother broke his arm once, our parents kept him out of sight until he was healed, telling us that no-one wanted to see a prince who wasn't perfect. But she didn't just injure herself. She hit her head and died almost instantly.'

Charlotte couldn't help the tears filling her eyes. She went to Salim and took his hands. They were cold.

Her voice was thick. 'You know it wasn't your fault…'

Salim let out a curt sound and took his hands out of hers. 'Wasn't it?'

'You were her brother—not her parent.'

Salim shook his head, as if determined not to let her absolve him. 'We were twins…we had a natural affinity… But somehow I didn't pick up on what was happening.'

'You didn't tell your parents? Your brother?'

A muscle in Salim's jaw ticked. 'I couldn't speak to Zafir. Sara and I…we'd all but blocked him out as soon as we could communicate with each other. We didn't need him. We didn't need anyone. Zafir seemed very remote to us. He was older. Serious. I did try to tell my father, but he just slapped me across the face and told me never to repeat such lies again. He said that Sara was dead and nothing could be done.'

'So you've kept that awful knowledge inside you for all these years…?'

He looked at her, and she shivered at the bleakness in his eyes.

'I made it my life's mission to get away from this place that never valued Sara and go after her abuser. I did. And now he's dead.'

Charlotte said faintly, 'He's the man you mentioned before?'

Salim nodded.

She sat down again, her legs feeling weak. 'Why didn't you bring him up on child abuse charges?'

'Because too much time had passed. There was no evidence. He actually laughed in my face when I mentioned my sister. So I got him the only way I could—by ruining him. Ruining him to the point where he took his own life.'

Charlotte's heart ached. '*He* took his life, Salim. Not you—no matter what you did.'

He looked at her, and opened his mouth as if he was going to argue with her, but at that moment there was a sound of movement nearby.

Salim tensed. 'Who's there?'

Zafir, his brother, stepped onto the path from around the corner. He looked as if he'd just been punched in the gut. Evidently he'd heard everything.

He looked at Salim—haunted, stricken. 'Why didn't you tell me, Salim? I would have done anything for you… She was my sister too…'

Emotion thickened between the two men, who stood facing each other, and Charlotte discreetly stepped back and away, sensing that this was a conversation that had been a long time coming and that they didn't require an audience.

Charlotte stole back along the path, her throat tight with emotion at the thought of Salim carrying the burden of his sister's trauma on his shoulders for all this time.

She found Kat pacing a little further along the path, clearly anxious.

When she saw Charlotte she hurried to meet her. 'What's happening? Zafir went storming after Salim, even though I told him I wasn't upset. I never should have meddled in Sara's garden...'

Charlotte took her hands. 'I think you did a beautiful thing, and I think Salim will recognise that when he's calmed down. He's talking to Zafir now... Your husband should be the one to explain things to you.'

Kat looked torn, but eventually she sighed and said, 'Fine. I should go and see how preparations are going for the banquet anyway. I just hope they're not tearing lumps out of each other.'

'I don't think they are,' Charlotte said weakly, mentally crossing her fingers and already feeling for Kat when she would learn the full story later.

When they reached the palace entrance Charlotte offered to help Kat, but the woman said an emphatic *no* and got a staff member to show Charlotte to her room, so she could rest before the banquet.

When Charlotte got to her room, Assa was laying out something gold and shimmery on the bed.

Charlotte went over and touched it reverently. 'What is this?'

Assa's voice was awed. 'It's a traditional Jandori kaftan, supplied by the queen as a gift to you. It was designed by one of their most famous designers. She has left a note saying that you don't have to feel obliged to wear it tonight, but that it's yours in any case.'

It looked too beautiful to be worn...the fabric as delicate as a butterfly's wing. The queen's generosity was humbling.

Charlotte looked at Assa. 'What do you think I should do?'

Assa was incredulous. 'You *have* to wear it, Miss McQuillan, you can't insult the queen.'

Charlotte smiled, glad to feel some lightness again.

Assa was backing away. 'I've unpacked all your things, and you should rest now. I'll be back to help you dress in a couple of hours.'

Charlotte was about to protest that she didn't need help, but she didn't have the heart to curtail Assa's obvious excitement. 'Thank you, Assa.'

Alone again, Charlotte took in the luxurious yet understated surroundings of her room. This was how Tabat palace could be some day, with some loving care.

And then Salim's sneering words came back to her, when he'd accused her of wanting to be a queen. Humiliation flooded her again at the thought that he might have seen something of her feelings on her face, like Kat had, and had seen all the way into her deepest secret yearnings for unconditional love and a family.

But did she secretly fantasise about being a queen?

Charlotte walked to the window and looked out over Jahor. The thought made her feel panicky, and yet she appreciated what Kat had said about feeling capable of anything with Zafir by her side.

Charlotte didn't want to be a queen, but to be Salim's queen… That was a different and far more dangerous dream.

She turned from the window in disgust at her mind's wanderings. Salim wasn't even going to be king for long…and she could appreciate fully now just why he'd resisted so forcibly. Even if she still didn't agree with him.

Charlotte had to remind herself that she was a temporary lover. Someone who had piqued his interest for a while because she was nothing like his usual women.

He was so proud. She knew he wouldn't relish having spilled his guts to her just now. But no doubt he felt that it was excusable, because soon she would be relegated to his past while he got on with his future. With or without Tabat.

And if he *did* decide to stay on as king then he would have to choose a suitable queen. Maybe someone from one of the tribes—a high-born tribal leader's daughter. Like the young woman who'd married that man. With her gorgeous kohled eyes and elaborate headdress. They would say *I marry you* three times to each other and then they would be married…

Charlotte cursed herself when she realised where her mind was going. She decided to take a refreshing shower and stripped off, pulling on a silk robe that was hanging behind the bathroom door.

She heard a noise in the bedroom and, thinking it would be Assa, went back out, stumbling to a halt when she saw that a door she hadn't even noticed was open between her room and another. And it was dominated by the man standing there, looking a little wild and feral.

Salim.

'You left.'

Charlotte was glad to see there were no obvious signs

of a fight on his face. She wondered how the exchange had gone with his brother.

'I didn't want to intrude.'

He made a sound at that—something between a laugh and a growl. He held out a hand. 'Come here. I need you.'

His voice resonated like a sensual command, deep inside her. She walked forward, very aware of the flimsiness of the silk robe against her naked body and of Salim's blue gaze on her.

She stopped in front of him. The air crackled between them, alive and electric.

'What do you need?' she asked, slightly breathlessly.

He looked even wilder up close, and it sent a shiver of awareness over Charlotte's skin. He put his hands on her hips and pulled her right into him. She gasped when she felt the thrust of his arousal against her belly.

'I need you,' he said thickly, 'and *this*.'

And then his mouth slammed down on hers and she was sucked into an immediate vortex of white heat and lust, making her legs turn to jelly.

Any of the remaining ice around her heart, that had protected her for years, was well and truly burnt away in this conflagration. How could she deny this man the release he sought in her arms when every bit of her ached to give him that release and then selfishly take her own...?

The surge of emotion Salim had felt when he'd seen Charlotte standing there in the silky robe was too much for him to take in. The need he'd felt for her was instantaneous and urgent. The need to lose himself in her until the pain went away.

She was arching her body into his and her mouth was so soft and sweet... He couldn't hold back even if he wanted to now. It was fast and furious, but somehow he managed to navigate them so that her back was against a wall.

They didn't even make it to the bed.

Salim lifted Charlotte so that her legs were wrapped around his waist, then pulled at her robe like an animal until she was bared and he could feast on her breasts, tugging first one and then the other nipple into his mouth, their pointed tips sending his arousal levels into orbit.

He somehow managed to pull up his own robe and she reached down between feverish kisses, finding his rock-hard erection and freeing him from the confines of his trousers.

For a second, while she held his body in her hand, he pulled back and looked at her. Her eyes were wide and glazed, her cheeks flushed. Hair tousled. His chest grew tight.

He removed her hand from his shaft and with less finesse than he'd ever shown in his life he found the heart of her body, where she was slick, tight and hot, and thrust up so deep that they both stopped breathing for a long moment.

When her hips moved against his he withdrew, before slamming back in. Her muscles clenched around him and he let loose the beast inside him until their skin glistened with sweat and he had nowhere else to go but to pull out before he lost all control, to spill his seed across her belly.

He'd never done that before, because he'd never not used protection, but right now he couldn't even drum up shock or recrimination.

Charlotte was looking at him wild-eyed, her hips still

moving against him, and to his shame and mortification he realised that she hadn't climaxed.

She was biting her lip as Salim lowered her to the floor, instructing roughly as he knelt before her, 'Put your leg over my shoulder.'

She did, and Salim pushed apart the robe even more, so that her body was bare apart from the flimsy belt dissecting her belly where he'd branded her. He spread apart her thighs and laved her body, hearing her sighs and moans, feeling her fist in his hair as he plunged two fingers inside her and found the sensitive nub of her pleasure, suckling on it remorselessly until she too fell apart, screaming her release.

When she was spent, Salim rested his head against her hips and for the first time in his life felt a sense of peace so profound that it silenced all the voices in his head.

Later, at the glittering banquet, Charlotte still felt flayed. They'd made love like two animals. Except she couldn't drum up any sense of shame or humiliation. It had felt wild and strangely cathartic. As if something had been burnt clean.

Incinerated, more like.

She caught Salim's eye now, across the table, and her inner muscles clenched. His mouth tipped up slightly on one side, as if he knew exactly what she was going through. She scowled at him and looked away, trying not to think about how he'd carried her into the shower afterwards and soaped her thoroughly—so thoroughly that she'd splintered to pieces *again* while he'd watched her with an intensity that she hadn't been able to escape.

Just before she'd returned to her room he had said, 'I didn't use protection...'

Her face had flamed as she'd thought how erotic it had felt to have him spend his release on her skin.

She'd hurriedly assured him, 'It'll be fine. I'm not at a dangerous part of my cycle'.

And she wasn't, so she could be relatively sure there would be no repercussions. But it had shocked her how easily she'd forgotten about safety. And how easily a very illicit image of a small, earnest dark-haired child with blue eyes had sneaked into her imagination.

The chatter of the banquet brought Charlotte back to the present moment and panic rose inside her.

Imagining babies and being queen... She was in so much deeper than she'd appreciated.

Salim was finding it hard not to stand up and walk around the vast banquet table to where Charlotte was sitting. Her face was turned away as she spoke to someone else, and one word thrummed in his blood: *mine*.

She was a vision in a gold kaftan, her hair piled high on her head. He'd noticed several men's gazes lingering on her all evening, and it had taken all his restraint not to drag her across the table and claim her.

His body was still heavy, replete with carnal satisfaction, and yet, as ever, there was an edge of growing hunger. Already. He observed her as dispassionately as he could, feeling a little desperate at the effect she had on him, but he couldn't be objective.

It struck him then, as he took in the delicate line of her jaw and aquiline profile... She looked regal. Maybe that awareness had precipitated his taunt earlier—that she wanted to be a queen. Suddenly Salim thought of how very perfect Charlotte would be as a queen, but she would have to be someone else's, wouldn't she?

She looked up at him now, and Salim felt pinned to

the spot. So much so that he had to look away—only to catch his brother's gaze at the head of the table. He felt something tight loosen inside him. Today had marked the very fragile start of a long overdue *rapprochement* with his brother, who hadn't done anything to deserve the distance Salim had put between them.

Salim could see now that for a long time he'd blamed Zafir for not protecting Sara, even though of course it wasn't his fault. But it had been easier to do that and push him away than to admit he was terrified of loving his brother and losing him, too.

Salim stood up and tapped his glass gently with a knife, causing everyone to stop and look at him. He made a short speech of thanks to his brother and his sister-in-law, to whom he'd apologised earlier, easing his conscience slightly. Then he found his gaze gravitating back to Charlotte's green one. She was looking at him with that unwavering regard that left him no place to hide.

He said, 'I pledge here, this evening, to do my very best to ensure a secure and successful future for Tabat.'

Everyone clapped and cheered, not realising that Salim's statement had been deliberately ambiguous. Charlotte did, though, and he saw the way she avoided his eye, as if she couldn't bear to look at him.

For the first time Salim felt more than just a twinge of conscience—he felt the inexorable rise of something he'd been trying to ignore for weeks. The realisation that he really meant what he'd just said, and that there was only one person he wanted to see guide Tabat into that secure and successful future...*him*.

He hadn't given so much as a thought to finding his replacement in the last couple of weeks...as if a part of him had already accepted the inevitable.

Shock at that revelation kept him rooted to the spot as everyone around him started to get up from their tables for the second part of the evening's celebrations, and he watched Charlotte—still avoiding his eye—as she got up too and turned away.

That broke him out of his stasis and he went after her, not really knowing what he was going to say when he got to her, but knowing that she was the only person he wanted to see.

CHAPTER NINE

'DANCE WITH ME?'

Charlotte stopped in her tracks at the familiar deep voice behind her. She considered saying *no* for a second and then thought, who would she be fooling?

No one.

And yet she couldn't let him see her for a moment.

It had hurt her more than she could say when he'd made that deliberately misleading comment just now, about Tabat. It had felt like a betrayal of everything she knew he stood for and a betrayal of this last week, when he'd been so inherently respectful of his people. His actions had spoken louder than his words. But he wasn't prepared to admit that.

The fact that she was the only one who knew that he had no intention of being King of Tabat felt like the heaviest burden now.

He came into her field of vision, holding out a hand. She looked up at him reluctantly and schooled her features as best she could. But she knew it was futile when she saw how that blue gaze narrowed on her face. He still looked as thoroughly disreputable as he had when she'd first seen him, in spite of the traditional robes. Wild curling hair. Stubbled jaw. Wicked eyes and an even more wicked mouth.

She wanted very much not to let Salim lead her into the other room, where slow, sexy jazz was playing. She wanted to resist his pull because it was fatal now, and she knew he'd destroy her without even realising what he was doing.

But she found her hand reaching for his even as she cursed herself for it.

Salim led her into the other room, where there were already couples dancing. King Zafir and Queen Kat were dancing, staring deep into each other's eyes, oblivious to their guests.

Salim expertly took Charlotte into his arms and started to lead her around the floor. The fact that he was such a graceful dancer when he strived so hard to pretend he wasn't a part of this world made something snap inside her.

She pulled back and looked up. 'Did you tell your brother that you're planning on abdicating?'

Salim seemed to sense her mood, and looked at her while still managing to guide her faultlessly around the dance floor. Charlotte wondered churlishly if the man displayed mediocrity in anything at all.

'No, I haven't—not yet.'

'Well, you should,' Charlotte said tartly, 'because he will have to deal with the fall-out in Tabat, his closest neighbour.'

Charlotte focused on a point somewhere over his shoulder acutely aware of his body next to hers, making her feel hot and jittery.

His chest rumbled against hers. 'You might be interested to know that I haven't told him because I haven't made a final decision yet.'

Charlotte's feet stopped and she looked at Salim. They'd halted in the middle of the floor.

'What are you saying?'

He didn't seem remotely fazed that they'd stopped dancing and were drawing interested glances.

He arched a brow. 'I would have thought that a woman of your considerable intelligence could work that one out.'

His mocking tone bounced off her. A surge of emotion was rising. 'You're really considering becoming king...and not abdicating?'

His mouth tipped up on one side in a wry smile. 'Is that so hard for you to contemplate?'

Charlotte shook her head, barely aware that they'd started moving again. 'Not at all. I just thought you'd made up your mind.'

'Well, I haven't yet...for sure. Let's just say that I've been persuaded to look at things a little differently in the past few weeks. And after meeting the people of Tabat...seeing it with my own eyes...it's a challenge that might not be as unpalatable as I'd thought.'

Charlotte looked up at Salim, unable to stop herself from saying huskily, 'You will be a great king, Salim. You deserve to serve them, and they deserve you.'

He grimaced slightly and said, 'That remains to be seen. And first I have to go to London tomorrow, for a function. Tabat's ambassador to Europe is holding a Christmas party in my honour. Come with me?'

Charlotte's insides clenched.

Christmas. London.

She wasn't ready to leave this part of the world, or Salim, but it would be an opportunity for her to remember who she was and where she came from. Her life wasn't here, with this man.

She had to protect herself. She had to move on.

She prayed that her emotions weren't showing on

her face when she looked up and said, as nonchalantly as she could, 'Yes, I'll come with you.'

She knew now that she wouldn't return to Tabat with Salim for the coronation—she couldn't. This was his destiny. But it was not hers. And it was time to remember that.

She ducked her head and turned her face to rest a cheek on his chest as they danced. And she closed her stinging eyes.

Driving through London and seeing the festive cheer of Christmas—streets thronged with slightly crazed-looking shoppers and the bright faces of children pressed up against shop windows to see the displays better— sent Charlotte on a brutal collision course with her past.

Usually by now, or around now, she would be holed up in her apartment, blocking it all out, pretending it wasn't happening. But now she welcomed it—because she'd been in danger of losing herself completely. Losing herself in a fantasy where she belonged to a man from an exotic land, full of vast deserts and beautiful nomadic people.

But the fact was that whatever affinity she felt for his land was as much of a fabrication as this forced festive cheer. And she most certainly didn't belong to Salim, no matter how intense their lovemaking had been just hours ago, as dawn had broken and the call to prayer had sounded over the sleepy city of Jahor.

She was like a miser, grabbing hold of as much as she could before it was all ripped away from her.

Charlotte couldn't help hearing Salim's phone conversations on the plane to England. He'd made no attempt to keep them private so she'd heard him instruct his staff to set up a hub office in Tabat palace from where he could oversee everything. And then he'd informed his legal team that he would be scheduling a significant meeting in the New Year, after his coronation.

A meeting to tell them that his business would be changing dramatically? That he would be scaling back to concentrate on his royal duties because he wouldn't be abdicating after all?

The speed with which he seemed to be happy to turn his life around in another direction would have made her dizzy if she hadn't got to know him by now, and to know his capabilities.

Charlotte couldn't help thinking that if he was indeed going to be king, then he would be looking for a queen to stand by his side. To have his heirs.

That made her think of Queen Kat, and how seamlessly and effortlessly she seemed to have become a beloved fixture in her adopted country. Because she was loved.

And that was the scariest revelation of all: falling for Salim had shown Charlotte that her parents' treatment of her hadn't damaged her as irrevocably as she'd believed. Somewhere deep inside her she'd nurtured a small seed of hope, and when Salim had come along it had burst into life before she could stop it.

'We're almost there.'

Salim's voice broke Charlotte out of her reverie and she looked at him. They were inching along in traffic on a street in Mayfair, near Tabat's embassy.

He was watching her, and she schooled her features, but not before he'd evidently seen something. 'You really do hate this time of year, don't you?'

'Yes,' she said tightly, relieved that he wasn't seeing anything deeper than that.

The car drew to a stop outside a stately house with

the Tabat flag flying on a pole outside. Seeing it made Charlotte feel even more homesick for a country where she'd only spent a few weeks.

She clambered out before Salim could come around to help her, and he looked at her as she preceded him up the steps and into the house.

The house was decorated for Christmas, making Charlotte feel a disjointed mixture of rejection and yearning. She felt churlish. A huge tree dominated the hall, and the smell of mulled wine and spices infused the air. It was surprisingly homely and familiar, and it was pushing about a million of her buttons.

Salim came to stand in front of her. 'The function will take place here, in the ceremonial ballroom. I have to attend a meeting with the ambassador first—I'll collect you at seven.'

'I'm sure I can make my own way there,' Charlotte responded quickly, wanting to put some distance between them. Especially when she felt so all over the place.

A familiar steely expression settled over Salim's face. 'I'll meet you at seven.'

Charlotte saw a smartly dressed older man waiting with her bags and forced a smile. 'Fine—if you insist.'

Salim watched as Charlotte disappeared up the main staircase behind the housekeeper. He frowned. It was almost as if she'd become a different person as soon as they'd landed in London. She'd hunched in on herself, as far away from him as possible in the back of the car, looking haunted and hunted.

He felt an uncharacteristic sense of concern…a compulsion to go after her and—what…? He cursed himself. Charlotte was just a lover. Different from any lover he'd had before, but that was all.

'Sire?'

Salim turned from where he'd been staring into space—which further irritated him. He didn't stand staring into space, wondering about a lover. Mooning after her.

'Yes?'

A secretary smiled and said, 'Let me show you to the ambassador's office.'

Salim resisted the urge to slide a finger under the collar of his shirt to ease the sense of constriction as he followed the older woman.

Taking him unawares was the strength of yearning he felt to be back in Tabat and looking out over the endless desert. He'd once dismissed it as a sandpit, but he now knew that it teemed with life. Humans and animals and plants. Majestic. Beholden to none but themselves...

How had he never really appreciated that before?

When Charlotte was alone in her luxurious suite of rooms she paced back and forth in front of the window, oblivious to her surroundings or the view of a private park outside.

What was she doing?

She should have insisted on making her way back to her own apartment from the airport, and she should have let Salim know that she was terminating her contract. After all, King Zafir had all but terminated it the previous evening.

He'd pulled her aside for a moment at the banquet and said, 'Thank you for everything you've done for my brother...'

Charlotte had fought not to go puce, and he'd continued before she could come up with a suitable response.

'I think you know by now as well as I do that Salim

follows his own path and seeks help from no one. He never has. However, I just wanted to say that as far as I'm concerned you've fulfilled the terms of our agreement. If you do decide to stay for the coronation, or longer than that, it'll be an agreement between you and my brother...'

Feeling a sense of grim fatalism, Charlotte went to the wardrobe, where the housekeeper had insisted on putting away her things. She was going to pack and tell Salim that she was leaving...or, better yet, leave now before he could come and get her.

But every thought left her head when she opened the wardrobe and saw a familiar silky green gown hanging inside.

Her heart spasmed. It was the gown Salim had sent to her room to wear at his party. The one she'd refused to go to. The one where she'd confronted him and he'd kissed her.

Barely daring to breathe, she took it out and held it up. It was as stunning as she remembered, falling in a swathe of silk from under the bust. A symphony of simplicity and elegance.

Charlotte cursed Assa—she must have seen it hanging up at the back of the wardrobe in Tabat and packed it.

A very rogue desire swept over her—*one more night with Salim*. One more night to indulge in fantasy and let herself believe that this was her world and he was her man.

She could protect herself, couldn't she? She wasn't so far gone that she wouldn't be able to pick up the pieces of her life again and pretend nothing had happened...

But the tightness around her heart told her otherwise. She felt icy for a second as the memory of her father's rejection came back—but surely, she reassured herself, this was totally different? She was an adult now, and if she walked away from Salim before he ended things then she'd be in control.

Charlotte knew she didn't have the strength to walk away. Not just yet.

One more night.

Salim was still trying to compose himself. But he felt feral. He was oblivious to the people around him because he was fixated on the woman on the other side of the room, talking to a group of people whom she apparently knew.

Why isn't she by my side? he asked himself again, irrationally.

The dress she was wearing… It was the green dress he'd ordered especially for her, describing what he'd wanted, the colour and style, to an amused French stylist friend of his who had teased him.

'This one must be special if you are ordering a dress to match her eyes…normally you send in your lovers to dress themselves.'

Salim had answered defensively, 'She's not my lover…'

But his friend had just laughed and said, 'Not yet.'

He'd been right about the colour. Even from here he could see that the green made her eyes look even mossier than usual. The dress was strapless and it clung to her breasts before falling in a swathe of silk to the floor.

But what was really exercising him was the fact that he'd never seen so much of her pale flesh exposed in public before. And now *everyone* could see the freckles that dusted her shoulders and arms.

Her hair was swept to one side, and one of the tuxedoed gentlemen near her had put a hand on her bare upper back.

Salim was moving forward before he realised that someone had put a hand on *his* arm and was saying, 'Please can I have a word?'

He curbed the urge to snarl, and stopped and looked. It was a young attractive woman, with dark eyes and hair, and for some reason a cold shiver went down his spine.

He recognised her at the same moment as she said, 'Maybe you don't know me. I'm Giovanna Scozza. My father was—'

'I know who your father was,' Salim said grimly, feeling slightly sick.

She took her hand from his arm and Salim could see the shadows in her eyes. She looked nervous.

'Do you think we could talk privately for a moment?'

She didn't have to say it, but Salim heard it. *Surely you can give me that?*

'Of course.'

He did owe her this—and more.

He instructed a staff member who was hovering nearby to ensure they weren't interrupted and he took her into a private study off the main ballroom.

Charlotte's skin crawled when Peter Harper put his hand on her back—*again*. Once again she moved subtly from underneath it, automatically seeking out Salim on the other side of the room.

Something sharp lanced her when she saw that he was talking to a tall and very beautiful young woman, with dramatic black hair, olive skin and dark eyes. The woman had put her hand on his arm.

He was looking at her as if...

Charlotte's heart hitched. She'd never seen him look so arrested before, and her insides turned to water.

This was it.

He might have looked at her as if he'd wanted to devour her on the spot just moments ago, but of course it wouldn't be long before he realised what he'd been missing.

She watched as he led the young woman into another room and a uniformed staff member took up a position outside, clearly under instructions not to let anyone disturb them.

Feeling sick, Charlotte made an excuse to the people she'd been talking to—fellow diplomatic staff—and escaped the crush of the crowd to find some air, some space.

When Salim re-emerged into the main room he was still reeling. He immediately looked for a familiar strawberry-blonde head and frowned when he couldn't spot her immediately. *Where was she?*

The group of men she'd been talking to had dispersed, and Salim cursed under his breath at the thought that she was in some more private space with the one who had been touching her.

People moved out of his way with widening eyes as he cut a swathe through the room, but he was unaware of the intensity of his expression.

He thought he saw a flash of green in the far corner and followed it, finding himself at the door of another private room much like the one he'd just left.

He went inside. A fire was blazing and the room's walls were lined with shelves filled with books. There was an elaborately decorated Christmas tree in the corner, but Salim only had eyes for the slender pale figure standing near the fire, watching him.

Immediately something in him eased. Even as desire swept through him, igniting his blood.

He closed the door behind him.

For a moment he forget what had just happened as he stalked towards her. 'Who were those men you were talking to?'

Her eyes looked very dark in this low light, and the flames of the fire picked out the red hues in her hair.

'Colleagues…from the diplomatic circuit.'

'Oh? It's a circuit?'

Her eyes glittered and he could see the pulse at the base of her neck throbbing.

Her voice was tight. 'Yes, Salim, it's a circuit much like any other. Much like the one you inhabit when you return to Europe—you know, where you run into old friends…even old *lovers*?'

For a second he didn't compute, and then he remembered.

His gaze narrowed. 'You saw me talking to Giovanna?'

Charlotte shrugged minutely, hating it that she couldn't hide her emotions better. 'Is that her name?'

Salim shook his head and a smile tipped up one corner of his wicked mouth. 'I do believe you're jealous.'

Charlotte's hands clenched into fists. Yes, she was jealous—and she hated it.

Innate honestly forced her to say, 'I never asked for this, Salim. I shouldn't really care less what you do, or who with, because I'm sure you couldn't give a damn what I do.'

She let out a choked sound of anger at herself and went to go past Salim and make her escape. But he caught her with a hand on her arm.

'On the contrary. I do give a damn. I didn't like seeing that man touching you. Who was he?'

Charlotte blinked up at Salim, momentarily distracted by the feral glitter in his eyes. She told herself it was just possessiveness, nothing more. 'It was no one... Peter Harper—a diplomat with the foreign office.'

She found herself melting at the thought that he could be jealous—but then she remembered seeing him disappearing into that room with that sultry dark-haired beauty and she pushed against his chest, forcing him back.

She stepped around him and folded her arms. 'Who was *she*?'

Salim ran a hand through his hair, making it even messier. He took off his jacket, throwing it onto a chair, and then he pulled off his bow tie. He turned around and Charlotte nearly took a step back at how wild he looked. Like a caged animal.

Eventually he said, 'Giovanna Scozza. That's who she was.'

Charlotte frowned. The name was somehow familiar.

Salim's face was stark. 'She's the eldest daughter of the man who abused Sara. The man I ruined in revenge.'

Charlotte went cold in spite of the heat from the fire. 'What did she want?'

'She asked if she could speak to me and I said yes, of course.' His eyes pinned Charlotte to the spot. 'Do you know I tried to absolve myself after he died by making sure that the family were taken care of financially?' He emitted a curt laugh.

Charlotte's heart turned over. *Of course he had.* 'No, you never mentioned that. Why did she want to see you?'

Salim sighed. 'She wanted to thank me for what I'd

done… She told me that he'd been an abusive father—'
He must have seen something on Charlotte's face, because he put out a hand and said, 'No, not *that*. Not with
his children, at least. But he was violent to them—and
their mother. It finally stopped when I went after him.
But not completely. He beat their mother the day before
he took his own life. She ended up in hospital. Giovanna
revealed that they'd finally told him they were going to
press charges against him. It was that more than anything else that made him take his own life—the thought
of the shame if it got out…'

Salim looked at Charlotte and his face was leached
of colour.

'She's effectively absolved me of guilt, but all I can
think of now is that if I'd done something sooner then
I might have spared them all—'

Charlotte stepped forward and put her hand to Salim's mouth, cutting off his words. She shook her head.
'It wasn't your responsibility, Salim. You can't blame
yourself for his sick violence, just like you can't blame
yourself for what happened to Sara.'

She took her hand down and stepped back, terrified
that her heightened emotions might give her away. She
had to be strong. Especially now.

But she couldn't help saying, 'You're free now,
Salim. Free to live out your destiny.'

'Free to live out your destiny.'

Charlotte's words impacted Salim deeply. As was
becoming dismayingly familiar with this woman, she
had somehow managed to slide right into the heart of
him and bear witness to the darkest parts of his soul
without turning from him in horror.

But then she turned and walked away, to pick up her
bag from a chair.

Something icy skated down Salim's spine.

When she turned around to face him again her face was a smooth mask. He might have imagined the emotion he'd seen shimmering in her eyes just now.

'Charlotte...?'

'I'm going to my room to pack.'

'But we're not leaving for Tabat till tomorrow afternoon—there's plenty of time.'

She looked straight at him. As if she was making herself do it. 'I'm not staying here.'

Salim moved towards her, ignoring the ominous feeling in his gut. 'If you hate being here this much we can leave tonight.'

She shook her head. 'It's not that. I'm not coming back to Tabat with you, Salim. Tonight or tomorrow.'

She turned to walk to the door and for a second Salim was incredulous. He wasn't even aware of moving until he was standing between her and the door, every muscle in his body taut. He didn't trust himself to touch her.

'What are you talking about, not coming back? You're working for me—or have you forgotten that pertinent detail?'

Charlotte let out a curt laugh that didn't sound like her. 'Working for you? *Now* I work for you? You know very well how to navigate in this milieu, Salim.' She waved a hand towards the noises coming from the other room. 'You really don't need my expertise. Your brother hired me, and he's released me from the contract so I'm choosing to go.'

Salim wanted to throttle his brother. 'He had no right to do that. But it doesn't matter because we've gone way beyond anything professional now. It's personal, Charlotte. '

She stepped back. Her face was flushed. She gestured between them. 'This was improbable from the start.'

Salim frowned. 'What are you talking about? We have amazing chemistry.'

'Chemistry, but that's all. How do you see this playing out, Salim?'

He didn't like the growing feeling of desperation. People obeyed him. Especially women.

But she never did, whispered a jeering voice.

He ignored it and bit out, 'I see this playing out by you coming back to Tabat with me, Charlotte.'

She shook her head. 'No, this ends here—now. If you need professional advice I can recommend someone, and as for the other...' She stopped and then said stiltedly, 'Well I'm sure you won't be alone for long.'

Salim was in uncharted territory. He knew if he touched Charlotte he could make her acquiesce in seconds, but something held him back. Some sense of self-preservation he'd never had to call on before.

'I told you I don't play games, Charlotte. If you leave here now I won't come after you. You know I want you. And I know you want me. Come back with me and we'll enjoy this for as long as it lasts.'

'I'm happy for it to end now.'

For the first time in his life Salim felt an urge to plead, or beg... And then a cold weight settled in his gut. *Not the first time.* He'd pleaded and begged with Sara, but she hadn't listened to him. She'd still left him.

The fact that he was thinking of Sara and Charlotte in the same vein was enough to make Salim take a step back.

She didn't mean that much to him. She couldn't.

It was lust. That was all. And the lust he felt for Charlotte would fade once she was out of sight and mind. Of course it would. Because that was all it was. No woman would ever make him beg again. Or feel the acute pain of grief or loss.

Salim felt cold as he said, 'You have a choice, Charlotte. Either you come back with me to Tabat and we pursue our mutual attraction to its natural end—and it *will* end—or you will never see me again.'

Charlotte had been teetering on the edge, fearing she was too weak to walk away from what Salim was offering even if it was finite. The lure to return to Tabat one final time with him had almost broken her. But then he'd said what he just had, and his words were hitting her like a million tiny pointed barbs.

It wasn't his voice she heard now—it was her father's.

'You have a choice here, Charlotte. Choose me and we leave together today. Choose your mother and you will never see me again.'

The toxic memory faded, but not the words.

She looked at Salim and felt her heart break into two pieces. She said quietly, 'Thank you for making it easy for me to walk away from you, Salim. Goodbye.'

And then she turned and left.

CHAPTER TEN

'WELL, WELL...APPARENTLY leopards *can* change their spots!'

Charlotte's hand was clenched so tightly around her glass of champagne that she had to relax it for fear of cracking the delicate crystal. A TV screen on mute was showing the news in a corner of the private club where the Christmas party she'd been invited to was taking place.

She hadn't wanted to come. It was Christmas Eve the following day, and she'd fully intended to be deep in hibernation mode by now. But knowing that the coronation was taking place today had driven her out in a kind of desperation to prove something to herself. That she was coping. That Christmas wasn't her *bête noir*. That the fact that man she loved was getting on with his life wasn't like a knife sliding between her ribs.

But every sparkling light, every Christmas tree and every group of carol singers she'd spotted on her way here had flayed her alive. It seemed to be particularly cruel that her heartbreak was coinciding with Christmas.

She watched now, helpless not to, as King Salim Al-Noury was crowned in the main ceremonial ballroom of the Tabat palace under the avid eyes of the world, eager to see this playboy prince brought to heel.

But, as Charlotte knew only too well, Salim would never be brought to heel. He would always retain that air of wild unpredictability and it would make him a great man.

He was almost unrecognisable. His hair had been cut militarily short and he was clean-shaven. His blue eyes stood out stark against his dark olive skin.

King Zafir was there, and Queen Kat. And Charlotte recognised some of the tribal leaders. And the young couple whose marriage she had witnessed in the tent. Then she saw Rafa and Assa in the crowd and she felt like crying.

The man next to her was blissfully oblivious to her turmoil. 'Didn't you just come back from Tabat?'

Charlotte forced a smile and tore her eyes away from the TV. She looked at the man and said, 'I was there just briefly. Now, if you'll excuse me, I have to be somewhere else.'

And that somewhere else was far away from here, where she could lick her wounds. Hopefully when she emerged again it would be spring and her heart might not still be weeping.

It was Christmas Day and there was nothing but endless grey skies and crashing waves. Not a Christmas tree in sight nor a twinkling light. But it wasn't much comfort to Charlotte as she turned and made her way down the long empty beach, back towards the cottage her grandmother had owned.

She'd left it to Charlotte in her will and it was in the furthest western reaches of Ireland, with literally nothing between it and America except the Atlantic ocean.

In the end she'd come here because she'd always found solace at her grandmother's cottage, even though

Charlotte had been only four or five when she'd died. The cottage felt like a link to someone she remembered vaguely as being very maternal, and Charlotte had used it as frequently as she could over the years.

She felt tears threaten and willed them back, refusing to give in to the weakness. She'd stockpiled enough cheesy DVDs to last her a week, and food to last her at least until the shops opened again. She was planning on curling up under her duvet and not emerging until it was at least January the sixth.

She pulled the zip of her parka up as far as she could and trudged back towards the cottage behind the sand dunes. As she got closer she frowned. There was smoke coming from the chimney that she could see peeping just above the dunes. She'd cleaned out the fire from the previous night and left it set, but she was certain she hadn't lit it.

She hurried her pace, cursing herself for not locking the door. But she'd always felt so safe here. The nearest neighbour was at least three miles away.

She was breathing hard by the time she came over the dune and stumbled to a stop.

There were vehicles outside the tiny cottage. A sleek four-by-four. And a van.

She saw a man come out dressed in overalls and ran down the other side of the dune, shouting, 'Hey! What on earth is going on?'

The man stopped and looked to the doorway, where someone else had just emerged. Charlotte followed his gaze and her heart stopped dead. *Salim.* Dressed in black jeans and a snug black Puffa jacket. He looked as out of place here as an exotic animal.

Another two men and a woman emerged from the cottage, and she could see him saying something to them and shaking one of the men's hands. They got into the van and another four-by-four she hadn't seen and drove away.

Somehow, fearing she was dreaming, Charlotte made her legs work and approached the cottage. Salim didn't disappear. He looked at her steadily, but when she got close she saw lines of strain around his mouth. And his eyes.

She shook her head. 'Salim...?'

He said nothing, just stood back and gestured with a hand for her to go into the cottage. As if it was his. As if it was perfectly normal.

She could smell the peat on the fire, and the distinctive scent grounded her in reality slightly. But when she stepped through the door reality slipped out of her grasp again.

Her jaw dropped. The fire was burning merrily. The entire open-plan downstairs area was decorated with holly and ivy and strings of lights. There was a smell of mulled wine and spices. Candles were burning, sending out a soft golden glow.

Charlotte looked into the kitchen and saw the table set with linen and cutlery finer than her grandmother had ever owned. The oven was on and she smelled cooking meat. Turkey. Food was piled up on the sideboard. Vegetables, wine, cake. Dessert. Fruit.

In the corner of the living room stood a Christmas tree bedecked with lights and glittering ornaments. There was one present under the tree—a small wrapped box.

Finally, Charlotte's heart seemed to kick into action. She looked at Salim. 'What is all this? Why are you here?'

Charlotte knew fatally that if this was some grand gesture just to get her back into his bed then she wouldn't have the strength to say no...

Salim came and stood in front of her and she couldn't take her eyes off his. They were so intense. She noticed now that he was pale.

'I did it because I wanted you to have a better memory of Christmas than the one that made you hate it so much…'

Her heart lurched. She was fragile enough to crumble at the slightest thing and this was pushing her to the edge.

'You didn't have to do that just because you felt sorry for me…'

He frowned. 'Sorry for you? The last thing I feel is sorry for you.'

Charlotte wanted to ask *why* again, but she wasn't sure she wanted to hear the answer. Or she did, but she was afraid it might not be what she wanted to hear.

'But…you were just crowned.' She struggled not to let her imagination run riot. She thought of something and sucked in a breath. 'You haven't abdicated already?'

He shook his head. 'I'm not going to abdicate.'

Relief flooded Charlotte, and for a moment she couldn't speak, she felt so overcome. Finally she managed to get out, 'I'm glad you decided not to.'

'But there is one thing that would make me consider it again.'

'What?'

'I can't do this without the right queen by my side. I've always believed I didn't need anyone, but recently I met someone and the truth is that I can't live without her. I was stupid enough to think that it was a temporary thing…lust. That it would burn itself out… But I was wrong. Dead wrong.'

Charlotte wasn't breathing.

Salim turned and went over to the tree, bent down to pick up the small wrapped present.

He came back and handed it to her. 'Open your present.'

She took it, but her hands were numb with shock and she couldn't work out how to take the paper off. Salim took it out of her hands and she noticed that they were shaking slightly. He ripped the paper and the bow off and handed it back to her.

It was a velvet box. Royal blue.

She opened it. It was a ring. A stunning emerald in an antique gold setting shone up at her from white silk.

She looked at Salim, hardly daring to ask the question even though he was looking at her in a way that set her insides alight with a very dangerous flame of hope.

'What does this mean?'

He came close and cupped her face. 'It means, my beautiful Charlotte McQuillan, of the silk shirts that drove me to distraction and still do, that I love you. I should never have let you walk away from me. I panicked. I was all but begging you to come back to Tabat with me and it reminded me of begging Sara...' He stopped and swallowed.

Charlotte put a trembling hand to Salim's jaw, scarcely able to believe what she was hearing.

He went on. 'I couldn't bear the thought of watching you walk away if I begged and you said no. I was a coward. It's taken me a lifetime to learn to love again, and I tried not to love you because I'm terrified of losing you, but it's too late... I know what you meant now, when you thanked me for making it easy for you to walk away. I was making you choose, just like your father made you choose.' He shook his head. 'I'm so sorry.'

Charlotte's emotion overflowed and tears slipped down her cheeks.

She whispered, 'I used it as an excuse not to tell you how I felt. I thought it would only last until you didn't want me any more. I had to reject you first.' Before she lost her nerve she said fervently, 'I love you, Salim. Even if you only think you love me and realise later—'

He stopped her words with his mouth. His kiss was explicit and thorough and when they came up for air Charlotte was welded to Salim's body, as close as she could get with several layers of clothing in the way.

As if realising this, he kicked the front door closed and started to take off their coats, dropping them where they stood. He took her in his arms again, the lines of strain on his face disappearing.

'I love you, Charlotte McQuillan. For ever. Come back to Tabat with me and help me to make it our home. The first real home we've ever had...'

She wound her arms around his neck, emotion making her chest ache. She nodded. 'Yes, I'd like that. I'd go to the ends of the world with you.'

They kissed again, with less desperate urgency this time, as if savouring this moment.

When Salim pulled back Charlotte said with a wobbly smile, 'I saw your coronation. You looked very regal.'

He looked serious. 'I needed you there. That's when I knew I couldn't do it without you.'

Charlotte's heart flipped.

And then it flipped again when he grimaced and said, 'I'm doing this all backwards...'

He went down on one knee and looked up at her. 'Will you marry me, Charlotte McQuillan?'

Love flooded her whole body and heart, healing all the past hurts. She said fervently, 'Yes, I will.'

'Now? Here?'

Charlotte blinked. 'But how?'

He stood up. 'You saw how it's done... We can say

the words to each other. Obviously we'll get married officially, but I don't want to waste any time.'

Charlotte's vision blurred and she nodded. 'Yes, I'd like that.'

Salim let her go and dragged a throw off the couch. He spread it on the floor and put down two cushions. He knelt on one and put out a hand for Charlotte to join him. She knelt in front of him on the other cushion, heard the fire crackling in the hearth.

He took the ring out of the box and joined their hands together in the prayer position. Then with his free hand he touched the tops of their fingers with the ring saying, 'I marry you…' three times, until he came to her ring finger and slid the ring home.

Then he took another ring out of his pocket, for him, and gave it to her. Charlotte felt the intensity of the moment as she copied his words, sliding his ring onto his finger and holding it there.

Salim interlaced their fingers. 'Now we're married.'

Charlotte said emotionally, 'For better or worse.'

'In sickness and in health.'

'Till death do us part.'

A huge smile split Salim's face, making him look young and free.

He reached for her. 'Come here, Queen Al-Noury, I need to make love to my wife.'

Charlotte went willingly, and it was much, much later when they finally emerged, sated and happy, to enjoy the first of many happy Christmases together.

Christmas Day, a year later. Tabat City.

'Three—two—one—ooh!'

Charlotte's breath caught along with the crowd's as

the massive Christmas tree in Tabat City's main square sparkled and shone when a thousand tiny lights came to life against the clear dusk-filled sky.

It was stunning, and she had been deeply moved when Rafa had come to tell her that the city's councillors had decided they wanted to do this to honour their English queen's heritage and make her feel at home.

'Is this okay?'

Charlotte heard the genuine concern in her husband's voice and felt him slide an arm around her waist. She nodded and bit her lip to contain her emotion, and then said, with a small hitch in her voice, 'It's more than okay... I think your antics last year cured me of any negative associations with Christmas for ever, and now this...'

He made a harrumphing sound and said, close to her ear, 'You talk of the deeply romantic actions of a man who had never done anything like that in his life.'

Charlotte turned her head to look up at her husband and remarked with a teasing smile, 'Indeed—who knew that behind the stone-cold heart of a playboy there was a romantic dying to be set free?'

He smiled and lifted her left hand, the light glinting off the solid gold eternity ring inlaid with tiny emeralds that he'd presented her with on the birth of their daughter, Sara, three months before. A month after Zafir and Kat—now both firm friends to Charlotte—had given birth to their son, Kalim.

The crowd cheered and clapped and the bundle in Charlotte's arms started to move, making small mewling sounds. She looked down into the just-awake eyes of her daughter and her heart squeezed.

Sara's eyes were still an indeterminate colour—somewhere between blue, grey and green. Charlotte secretly hoped they'd be blue, taking after her father and the beloved aunt they'd named her for. She would be the first Queen of Tabat, if she so wished. And if she didn't wish it, then that would be ok too.

Salim had vowed to do everything in his power to ensure the rules of succession were as democratic as possible so no child of theirs would be forced to take on a role they didn't want.

Sara's garden in Jahor was now a much loved and visited site—a place of peace and contemplation for anyone who had suffered loss. In the past year Salim had done a lot of healing, together with his brother, and he'd truly come into his own. He was the beloved king, who was slowly but surely bringing his country into a new future.

He had set up a foundation to take care of all his myriad business concerns, run now by carefully hand-picked staff. And he was also setting up the first digital hub in this part of the world, determined not to let his tech investments fall by the wayside. There was an air of industry and optimism throughout Tabat now, and tourism was rocketing.

Kat had been invaluable to Charlotte—helping to ease her into the intimidating role of queen—but to her relief the people of Tabat had welcomed her with un-conditional acceptance and affection. The birth of their daughter had helped unite the country even more, and Charlotte's favourite moments were those spent with the nomadic tribes out in the far reaches of the end-less desert.

Salim saw the telltale brightness in his wife's eyes as she looked out over the crowd and felt an answer-ing surge of emotion. He still couldn't believe where he was now—*who* he was. How rich his life was. And how poor it would have been if he hadn't finally embraced his destiny.

He deftly took Sara from Charlotte's arms, cradling her against his chest. His daughter gazed up at him with the unblinking trust and love that humbled him every time he looked at her.

They waved for the few more requisite minutes, and as the crowd's cheers died down and they finally started to disperse Charlotte slid her arm around his waist.

He looked down at her. She smiled. 'Home?'

Salim's heart felt so full it might burst. He nodded and said emotionally, 'Yes, *home.*'

And together they went back to their palace, savouring every moment of joy and happiness their love brought them, because they both knew the value of learning to trust and love again.

* * * * *

If you enjoyed
A CHRISTMAS BRIDE FOR THE KING
you're in luck! The first part of Abby Green's
RULERS OF THE DESERT *duet*
is ready and waiting for you to read!
A DIAMOND FOR THE SHEIKH'S MISTRESS

And also by Abby Green...
CLAIMED FOR THE DE CARILLO TWINS
MARRIED FOR THE TYCOON'S EMPIRE
All available now!

MILLS & BOON®

MODERN™

POWER, PASSION AND IRRESISTIBLE TEMPTATION

MILLS & BOON®

EXCLUSIVE EXTRACT

Leonidas Betancur was presumed dead after a plane crash, and he cannot recall the vows he made to his bride Susannah four years ago. But once tracked down, his memories resurface – and he's ready to collect his belated wedding night! Susannah wants Leonidas to reclaim his empire and free her of his legacy. But dangerously attractive Leonidas steals her innocence with a touch… And the consequences of their passion will bind them together for ever!

Read on for a sneak preview of Caitlin Crews' next story
A BABY TO BIND HIS BRIDE
One Night With Consequences

There was a discreet knock on the paneled door and the doctor stepped back into the room.

"Congratulations, *madame*, *monsieur*," the doctor said, nodding at each of them in turn while Susannah's breath caught in her throat. "The test is positive. You are indeed pregnant, as you suspected."

She barely noticed when Leonidas escorted the doctor from the room. He could have been gone for hours. When he returned he shut the door behind him, enclosing them in the salon that had seemed spacious before, and that was when Susannah walked stiffly around the settee to sit on it.

His dark, tawny gaze had changed, she noticed. It had gone molten. He still held himself still, though she could tell the difference in that, too. It was as if an electrical current ran through him now, charging the air all around him even while his mouth remained in an unsmiling line.

And he looked at her as if she was naked. Stripped. Flesh and bone with nothing left to hide.

"Is it so bad, then?" he asked in a mild sort of tone she didn't believe at all.

Susannah's chest was so heavy, and she couldn't tell if it was the crushing weight of misery or something far more dangerous. She held her belly with one hand as if it was already sticking out. As if the baby might start kicking at any second.

"The Betancur family is a cage," she told him, or the parquet floor beneath the area rug that stretched out in front of the fireplace, and it cost her to speak so precisely. So matter-of-factly. "I don't want to live in a cage. There must be options."

"I am not a cage," Leonidas said with quiet certainty. "The Betancur name has drawbacks, it is true, and most of them were at that gala tonight. But it is also not a cage. On the contrary. I own enough of the world that it is for all intents and purposes yours now. Literally."

"I don't want the world." She didn't realize she'd shot to her feet until she was taking a step toward him, very much as if she thought she might take a swing at him next. As if she'd dare. "I don't need you. I don't *want* you. I want to be free."

He took her face in his hands, holding her fast, and this close his eyes were a storm. Ink dark with gold like lightning, and she felt the buzz of it. Everywhere.

"This is as close as you're going to get, little one," he told her, the sound of that same madness in his gaze, his voice.

And then he claimed her mouth with his.

Don't miss
A BABY TO BIND HIS BRIDE
By Caitlin Crews

Available January 2018
www.millsandboon.co.uk

YOU LOVE

RO

RO

For exclu
and spec